Monica Roe

FARRAR STRAUS GIROUX

NEW YORK

To Raven,
my gunpowder girl . . .
and to every other kid
determined to do
things their way

Farrar Straus Giroux Books for Young Readers
An imprint of Macmillan Children's Publishing Group, LLC
120 Broadway, New York, NY 10271
mackids.com

The definition of *testudo* is quoted from *Merriam-Webster*.

Our books may be purchased in bulk for promotional, educational, or business use. Please contact your local bookseller or the Macmillan Corporate and Premium Sales Department at (800) 221-7945 ext. 5442 or by email at MacmillanSpecialMarkets@macmillan.com.

Library of Congress Cataloging-in-Publication Data is available.

First edition, 2022
Book design by Mallory Grigg
Printed in the United States of America by LSC Communications,
Harrisonburg, Virginia

ISBN 978-0-374-38865-2 (hardcover)
1 3 5 7 9 10 8 6 4 2

1

Catching Air, Eating Sand

Ale heaves the ramp over the sandy, stubbly grass field that lies between her place and ours. "Your dad's gonna kill us, Em," she says cheerfully.

"Only if he catches us." I tighten my battered helmet, check my knee and elbow pads, and glance at the ramp. "Little closer, okay?"

Ale groans. Her shiny, dark braid swings over her shoulder as she shoves the ramp until it's right up against the bottom of the six-foot-high quarter-pipe. It's a kicker—a small, movable ramp that bikers and boarders use to launch themselves into the air.

Which is the plan.

Ale flips her braid back and shakes her sore arms. "That good?"

"Perfect." I nailed riding down the quarter-pipe months ago, but the field's too bumpy for me to get enough speed to hit the kicker from the ground. So I decided to try combining the two. Problem solved. I hope. "Boost, please!"

"Em, you sure about this?" Ale's hesitation is so brief it's almost invisible. When I give her a look, she laughs. "Okay, okay. But promise you won't make me have to explain to your dad how you got stuck headfirst in a round bale."

"Deal," I tell her, and Ale helps get me and my ride to the top of the quarter-pipe. For all his worry now, Dad used to be on this thing every weekend, too. Built it himself—one part tree stand, two parts salvaged plywood, three parts other random junk. Skateboards, motocross, he did it all—it's no secret where I got my love of speed.

We used to be out here together, instead of me having to sneak around.

I pull on my padded gloves, bring my front wheels to the edge, and breathe. The view from the top of a drop—even a basic one like this—gets me going every time. Those tadpoles swimming in my chest and the sweat on my palms are the best kind of rush. Now that added jump waiting at the bottom makes my guts fizz like I ate a handful of live bees and chased them with a bottle of Coke.

Right. Let's *do* this.

Helmet—double-check.

Mouth guard—check.

Visor—down.

Pads—tight.

I restrap my gloves and grip my wheel rims. *Breathe.* Dad won't be home from class for at least an hour. A good daughter wouldn't want her father to worry.

All Dad's ramps and jumps and angled steel grind rails made from old I beams have just been sitting out here getting dusty since he gave it all up. *Someone* has to use them.

Three, two, one . . . *drop!*

Whoosh. Wheels. Adrenaline.

One glorious, wind-rushing moment.

I lean. Find that perfect balance point. Hit the landing.

Then my wheels skid sideways, spinning me out. *Ow.*

Ale runs over. "You did it!" she yells. "Sort of. What's my name?"

I push up, spitting out a mouthful of the sand that padded my wipeout, and squint at the hand she's waving in my face. "Um . . . Ale? Rhymes with *sail*?" This is how people who don't know her usually say her nickname. It's actually pronounced *Ah-lay.*

"Ha-ha," she says.

"Just kidding." I tell Ale to grab a wheel, and we get me rocked upright.

She grins. "That was so cool."

It totally was, even though I dumped at the end. Now that Dad's so busy fixing cars all day, *and* running to night class three times a week, *and* taking in extra work here at his home shop . . . what he doesn't know won't even worry him.

I *will* stick that landing.

Then I feel my left handrim wobble. "Crap."

Correction—I'll stick that landing if my raggedy wheelchair doesn't fall apart on me first. I spin the wheel a few times, testing the handrim—yep. Definitely a loose screw and some bent metal.

"You want to try and fix it?" Ale asks. I keep my repair kit right in my top desk drawer, and basic patch jobs are easy enough. I'm tempted. After hitting that air once, I'm totally hungry for more. But Dad won't be *that* late.

"Let's call it for today," I decide. "Got a few orders backed up, anyway."

Sidewalks aren't exactly a thing out where we live, but my yard has more square feet of pavement than anywhere this side of the Dollar General parking lot. Ale's family owns a paving company, and my dad swapped them two years of free truck maintenance to pour glassy smooth walkways from our house to his shop and a bunch of places in between. One even cuts through the scrubby patch of woods to Ale's place.

We hurry up the long ramp to my porch and hurtle inside so fast the Spanish moss wreath Nonny made almost falls off the front door. If my grandmother saw me now, she'd make a sour-lemon face and predict I'll crash across the living room and through the opposite wall one day. *It's a double-wide, Nonny*, I giggle under my breath, imagining her right here, *not a cardboard box*. Nonny would drop her dentures if she'd seen my little sand-eating stunt back there. *Especially* if she saw how we got me and my chair up that quarter-pipe in the first place. There's a metal work platform—a set of two portable steps with a railing—that Dad attached to the backside of the quarter-pipe back when we used to ride this ramp together. I can get up it myself, though it goes a lot faster with Ale there to pass up my chair instead of just hauling it up with the cobbled-together pulley system I usually use when I'm doing it solo.

I've got my system down, although Nonny—and a whole lot of other folks—would still insist I have no business doing it. But I'm used to dealing with minor freak-outs whenever I do stuff that's a little risky. Besides, what other people think I can or can't do doesn't matter.

These are the things that matter.

I'm Emelyn Ethrige. I'm twelve and a half years old. Alejandra Che is my best friend.

I like Flamin' Hot Cheetos.

And I *love* speed.

2

Embroidered Cusswords?

Inside, I clean the road rash on my arm and make sure I'm not banged up anyplace else, and Ale raids the kitchen cabinets for some snacks. I collect Dad's laptop from the coffee table. Then we head to my room, and I line up a playlist while Ale checks orders in our online shop.

"I've got two Spanish moss and one pine cone box," she announces. Then she clicks over to my shop. "And you've got two fatwoods and another bag."

We may live out in the middle of Carolina scrubland, where the soil looks more like beach sand and everything green turns fried-up brown by early July, but Ale and I are experts at selling what we scavenge or make. Because we are entrepreneurs with *goals*.

Ale opens my closet to check inventory. We keep our

supplies in my room, because Ale's two little brothers cannot be trusted to keep their mitts to themselves.

"We've got moss," she reports, "and wood bundles, but we need more cones."

The best part about our business is that most of what we sell is scrounged from right outside. There are ten acres between our places, half covered in scrubby loblolly and longleaf pines that drop endless perfect cones. The Spanish moss grows on most everything that doesn't move, and tons of people—mostly in cities where trees don't exist, I guess—buy this stuff.

"If you go grab some," I tell Ale, "I'll do the moss and the fatwoods."

Ale grabs a bucket and runs outside while I get started. The moss orders are simple—wrestle the long, twisty strings into small plastic bags, put them in pad-ded envelopes, add addresses, and record the sale. Next, the fatwood.

Fatwood bundles are basically sticks. But not just any sticks—these are special, pitch-soaked wood that make it super easy to light a fire. You just start with a small chunk of stump, carefully split off thin, six-inch lengths, tie up a bunch of them with a ribbon or pretty fabric—instant rustic gift! Since Ale's not back when I finish the four packages, I fire up the sewing machine and work on my bag orders.

The custom-made wheelchair bags don't exactly fit our theme and sort of happened by accident. When I started carrying a lot of books for school, regular backpacks always got too full. When I'd hang them behind my chair, they'd sometimes pull my balance backward or fall off the handgrips. So last spring I designed my own schoolbags—lightweight, rugged, made to stay perfectly on the back or side of a chair.

They turned out super well, and when Ale asked if other people might buy them, I made a few and put them in the shop.

People bought them. It took some trial and error, but now my bags are lightweight and customizable for any type of chair—manual, power, even walkers. Plus, they never fall open and dump your books and papers all over.

I get to work on a tie-dye bag for Angus1 from Seattle, stitching the two lightning bolts he wants sewn on in metallic gold thread. My machine isn't fancy but does decent embroidery, and it has a start/stop switch instead of a foot pedal, which is key. Sewing is slow and precise—not my biggest strengths. Time sewing bags is time I'm not practicing jumps, but it's going to get me to my goals.

Speaking of that, I'd better head out to the workshop later and borrow Dad's air compressor to blow the grass and dirt out of my wheels before he gets home.

Next is a smaller Avengers print bag for a girl in North Dakota. That one will have extra pockets, which will take longer, so I put it off for this weekend. Then I read the new order, from an old lady in Alaska. She wants a standard-size manual chair bag in pink plaid. With lace trim. Her profile seems interesting, though—pictures of her fishing and playing guitar and other cool things like that. Anyone who lives on an Alaskan island must be impressive. I open my order log to add it to the list.

- **Angus1: medium handlebar bag, tie-dye, two gold lightning bolts. <u>Status: Ready to ship.</u>**
- **NotYourPrairiePrincess04: small side bag, Avengers print, blue/red ribbon ties. <u>Status: Finish this weekend.</u>**

I start entering AK_SalmonGranny's order and see something I missed earlier. Not only does she want ugly plaid and lace on her bag, she also wants a . . . personal message.

Keep staring, sweetie . . . I might do a trick.

Only it doesn't say *sweetie.* It says another s-word. One I'm not allowed to say.

I double-check AK_SalmonGranny's profile. Little old lady, blue-framed wheelchair, sitting on a wooden dock and holding a huge silver fish by the tail.

Grandmothers must be different in Alaska.

"Sorry I took so long!" Ale bursts in with a loaded bucket in one hand and a bag in the other. "I ran home for these." She lifts the bag. "How's it going?"

I point to AK_SalmonGranny's order details. Ale reads it and bursts out laughing. "You going to do it?"

"It's a little . . . aggressive?" I know Dad wouldn't love the idea of me using cusswords. Even just sewed-on ones.

Ale sets down the bucket, pops a piece of gum into her mouth, and hands me one. "You hate when people stare at your chair, too."

"Of course." Who doesn't?

Dad texts me then, telling me he's going to be later than he planned.

"I say do it," Ale declares. "That lady seems cool. My abuela would never order something like that."

"Can you imagine Nonny doing it?" I say, and we both crack up.

"Besides," she says, "money is money, right?"

"Money is money," I agree. "But I'll have to think about this one."

"Enough business for now. Here." Ale thrusts the bag she's still holding at me. I dump it on the bed, and a silky, gorgeous shimmer of cloth and ribbon slithers out.

"I love you forever." I pick out some shiny black and red pieces that will be perfect for my pirate fairy costume. There's a big outdoor fairy festival every year two towns over, and we've been going together since our moms used to take us in our strollers. We design our costumes way in advance.

Ale pulls some ribbons from the pile and weaves them into her long braid, then lays a few combinations on the bedspread. "You better! I had to fend off my sisters for these." Ale's aunt Rosaria makes custom dresses for weddings and First Communions and quinceañeras. Ale and her sisters and cousins all take turns getting the leftover scraps of expensive fabric and fancy ribbon. Whenever it's Ale's turn, she brings the haul over, and we work on costumes for ourselves.

"You still going with the bee fairy?" I ask, looking at her black, gold, and white choices.

"What else?" Ale holds two bits of gold ribbon over her head like antennae. "If business keeps up, I might get my new hive by spring instead of next summer."

Ale's all about bees. She's determined to become a Master Beekeeper (only she calls it Mistress High Beekeeper) before she turns sixteen. It sounds like a lifetime to me, but Ale insists it's basically impossible to do that quickly. Which means, of course, that she will.

"That's amazing!" Ale's been saving her profits for a huge, super-fancy hive that looks like a tiny house—shingled roof, wooden windows, copper accents, the works. It's like a designer dollhouse built for bees—and crazy expensive. For a bee house, anyway. I can't judge, though, since my goal will cost even more than the honeybee mansion.

That gets me thinking about what I'm saving for, so I roll to my wall chart and admire the numbers on the little printed thermometer stretching up the wall to my ultimate goal—and the picture taped beside it. As soon as these latest orders go out, I'll add some more red to the thermometer and be that much closer to my dream.

A high-end, multi-link-suspension stunt chair.

Coil-over shocks. Floating rear axle. Skate wheels.

Built for WCMX. The ultimate ride. Then I'll *finally* be able to get serious about skating without worrying about tearing up my regular wheels all the time.

Because when I'm skating, flying free . . . that's when I can truly be *me*.

3

Emmie Surprise

My growling stomach reminds me to start dinner after a while, so Ale brings the laptop to the kitchen and plays videos while I make Emmie Surprise, my second-best recipe. I last until I've cooked the pasta and peas. Once the ground turkey's browning in the pan, I crack.

"Okay, enough," I tell her. "One more beekeeping video and I'm in Nightmare City."

"How else am I supposed to learn different types of swarming behavior?" Ale protests, but, as usual, she eventually gives up the keyboard. I click right off the creepy bee-swarm close-up and open the newest Wheelz video instead.

He starts out freestyling at a regular skate park, flipping his chair and balancing on two hands, then one hand at the top rim of the half-pipe before plunging down the concrete ramp. It's all set to bass-heavy music that gets right into my bones.

The video cuts to a packed stadium with a massive jump in the middle. Wheelz pulls on his helmet and flings his chair down the drop like an avalanche. He catches air, does a *front flip* . . . and lands wheels-down. The crowd loses its mind.

I get chills.

"Wow," Ale breathes, then frowns at my chair. "Yeah, we *definitely* need to get you those new wheels."

"Almost thirty percent there," I remind her.

I've been following WCMX athletes since before I popped my first wheelie. The way they hurtle down jumps and spiral through the air is indescribable. They can wipe out ten times, then nail the eleventh.

And those chairs—rugged, sleek, practically indestructible—are a dream.

My dream.

With wheels like that and about a million hours of practice, I'll be unstoppable.

I could watch forever, but the turkey's popping in the pan. I remind myself to study his landing again later and finish dinner. Ale's mom calls, so she heads home, and I go back out to the shop to fire up the air compressor and blow the grass and dirt from my wheels. Then I come inside to put the dinner stuff away.

As I shut the fridge back in the kitchen, my shoulder

stings where I landed on it earlier. I decide to leave AK_SalmonGranny's cusswords for now and fix my rim instead.

I grab my tools from my room but quickly realize it's worse than I thought. Besides the loose handrim, one armrest is bent and won't latch tight. Nothing Dad can't fix, but he'll have to use the vise in the garage to straighten it.

When Dad gets home, I can tell he's beat by the way his footsteps drag up the ramp.

"Sorry I'm so late, Emms." He pulls off his work boots and goes to the sink to scrub up.

"No worries. We got a lot done on our costumes. How was studying?"

Dad groans. "Okay," he says. "Then I stopped at your grandparents' to change their oil."

I know how that went. Pop-Pop is the best, but Nonny never met a family member she couldn't dis-approve of.

Dad frowns. "What happened to your arm?"

I yank my sleeve over the telltale scrapes. "Nothing."

"Pretty scuffed-up nothing." Dad pushes my sleeve back and sighs when he sees my arm. "Let me guess. You were on the ramp."

"Maybeeeee."

"Emmie!" Dad plops into his recliner. "What did we talk about?"

"I know, I know—but look! Dinner!" I dish up a bowl of Emmie Surprise and balance it in my lap, swiping a fork from the drawer on the fly. "Here. You're always more reasonable when you're not hangry."

"Emelyn, we talked about this." Dad tries to glare at me, but he's fighting a smile, which he hides behind a huge bite of food. "I don't want you on that ramp. Especially not by yourself."

"Yeah, but how else can I get good enough for the ramp besides practicing on it?" Calm and sensible—with added charm—usually gets me what I want. Then I pull out the secret weapon.

"Who always says four wheels don't equal a free ride?"

Dad freezes mid-swallow, and I know I've got him.

Ever since the beginning—when the hospital folks broke the news that Baby Emmie's spinal cord left the factory with a design glitch—Mom and Dad never expected me to do less than other kids and never let anyone get away with acting like I was some miracle for getting out of bed and making it to the fridge each morning. They put me on wheels, had me popping curbs by the time I was six, and let me fly down baby-size ramps soon after.

Plus, Dad loves speed as much as me. He gave up trail racing dirt bikes after Mom died two years ago, but I know how much he still misses it.

"You do yourself any damage I should know about?" he asks, and I know I'm in the clear.

"Just a scuff or two!" I assure him, shuttling plates to the dishwasher. Time to change the subject. "Is your class interesting this semester?"

"It is, actually," he admits, kicking up his footrest and getting comfy. "If I didn't have to worry about passing, I think I could even like it."

"You'll pass," I tell him. It's been harder without Mom here to help him study, but he can do it.

"Hope you're right," he says. "Now, about those scrapes . . ."

"Let me show you my costume first!" Before Dad can answer, I zip down the hall to my bedroom and come back with my half-finished pirate fairy getup.

"Very scoundrelly." He holds up the dress to admire the raggedy stripes along the hem. "Your mom might have fought you for this one."

"She'd have let me have a sword, too," I hint.

"Nice try. Your mom would have kept the sword for herself."

Mom loved the Fairy Festival. Dad, on the other hand, always had to be dragged along. Mom usually won by threatening to seize control of all music played at home for a month if he tried to weasel out. Dad would cave, grumbling about "artsy-freaky, nerdy-pirate music" the whole time. I don't think he really minded, though he'd never be anything but a plain old blacksmith or woodcutter (boring old chainsaw chaps and a hatchet in his belt).

Dad has no poetry in his soul, but he always liked that Mom did—even if he pretended not to. Now that it's only us two, Dad always marks the festival on the calendar and never complains about going. I guess it's sort of how I always hated to do dishes or clean the bathrooms, but now I do it all the time without being asked.

Dad seems to have forgotten the ramp, so I wait on telling him about the chair repairs for now. He makes popcorn our favorite way—covered in melted butter and spicy Old Bay Seasoning—and we watch a movie. It's bedtime then, so I head to my room.

When he comes in about fifteen minutes later to shoo me off the tablet and call lights-out, he studies my wall chart. "You're going wide open on this, Emms. Proud of you."

I feel a rush of pride. "You're not the only one who

likes nice wheels," I joke. He laughs and gives me a quick kiss on the head.

"Sleep tight." He heads for the door. Then he pauses in the doorway, and when he turns back around, his face looks sharper.

"Emmie," he says. "I want you to stay off that ramp."

I start to make a joke, deflect like I always do, but Dad frowns.

"I'm not messing around. Consider this an official warning."

I pretend-salute him and half hide a giggle, waiting for him to crack a smile, too.

Instead, his frown turns into a scowl. "Don't sass me, kiddo."

Then he flicks off the light and walks out before I can say anything at all.

What the heck?

I stay awake a long time after that.

Dad never used to *forbid* things. He was my biggest cheerleader—my partner in high-speed mischief. Since Mom's been gone, he's so . . . *different*. Cautious. Scared, even. Sometimes it almost feels like he wants me to be scared, too. I don't understand it.

Beams from the full moon leak through my window and hit my cluttered desk, painting cool light over the jumble of pine cones, fabric scraps, and that letter from school I conveniently forgot to show Dad.

Dad used to call full moons Emmie's Moon. *Come on, Emms!* he'd sing, swinging me out of my tiny chair and running outside. *Pinch that moon, girl!* He'd toss me over his head, and I'd pretend to pinch the moon between my fingertips.

I try to sleep, but my thoughts won't slow down. Dad used to believe I could do anything. Now it feels like he doesn't believe I can pinch the moon anymore.

Even worse, sometimes it feels like he'd rather I didn't even try.

4

Princes and Clowns

"You got everything?" Dad asks again as he idles his pickup in front of the school.

"Yep." I pretend to hand over my schoolbag. "Unless you want to throw in a bottle, diapers, and a pacifier." I'm still frustrated about Dad's "warning" last night, but after sleeping on it, I think he must have been overtired and stressed over being so busy with everything.

"Ha-ha." He flicks my arm and jumps out to grab my wheels from the flatbed.

I shouldn't tease him when all that coffee he just slurped on the twenty-minute drive to school hasn't kicked in. He's been pulling triple duty lately—I can cut him a break or two.

"Don't fall asleep driving someone else's wheels," I joke as I swing down from the truck into my chair.

"Don't flatten anyone with yours," Dad fires back, handing me my bag. "Love you, Emms."

"Back at you." Dad drives off, and I join the sea of backpacks and backsides flowing into E. L. Pinckney Junior High. I scan the crowd for my friends. Ale and me share a ride a few days a week, but today she and her mom met one of her aunties for early-early breakfast before school.

Just like back at the elementary building, there's no automatic door, but I'm pretty good at popping a door open fast enough to get my front wheels through and wriggle my way inside. As I grab the door handle, a big hand darts out and snatches it.

"Allow me, my dear." The hand whips the door open so fast it almost whacks a guy in a camo T-shirt in the nose.

It's our principal, Dr. Grayling—who I sometimes think of as Fish, because talking to him can be like trying to get a fish off the line—you never quite know which way things will flip, and it all feels a little slippery. Before I can stop him, he grabs my chair and rolls me through.

Fish and me are still sizing each other up. He started at ELP last spring, and I doubt he's had a student who used wheels before—at least not one who doesn't usually need extra help. I'm fine asking for help when I need it, but he never really asks first.

Ale and Tina shove their way through the crowd then, and Dr. Grayling goes back to fussing at everyone to *stop shuffling and get to your classes, already.*

"I see Fish still thinks you can't start the day without him," Ale says when we're halfway down the hall.

Tina rolls her eyes. "My mom said he was the same way when she worked with him. Obsessed with rules and into everybody's business." Tina's mom works over in Harper County, where Fish was principal up until last year. They can have him back, if you ask me.

The bell rings then, and we hustle to our homerooms. This school's a lot more spread out than K–6 was, which is fine by me. There are a lot more kids here, too, since three elementary schools combine once we get to junior high. We're only a couple weeks into the school year, but so far seventh grade is everything I hoped for. Changing classes, more freedom—it all feels just a little bigger and more exciting. I think it's only going to get better, even though I've always been more into speed than studying.

The three of us meet back up at lunch and take our food to the outdoor courtyard where we can each report how things are going.

"Same old, same old," Ale declares, digging into her

leftover pupusas. "Seventh grade has turned out to be as simple as sixth. Except my science teacher had robotics club sign-ups, which sounds slightly cool."

Tina and I pretend to die of boredom, but we're proud of how smart she is. If we lived someplace else, Ale would totally be in some fancy smart-kid school, and I'd probably be on some hotshot wheelchair-sports team by now.

Then Tina's eyes narrow. "My girls," she says, "I believe we are under surveillance."

Ale and I follow her gaze across the courtyard, where a few guys are messing with a basketball and sneaking glances our way. I haven't given them much thought since school started—pretty much the same set of goofballs I remember from last year. Then Devontae Washington comes around the corner and joins them.

Devontae is *definitely* not the same. He's shot up over the summer and looks even taller with those fancy-stitched cowboy boots he's always wearing. A belt buckle glitters against his jeans, surely a prize from his latest win.

Devontae's a rodeo prince. Boy's been horse crazy since kindergarten, where the busted-up school playground had some battered metal animals on coiled springs. Every recess, Devontae would race to claim this chipped old aqua pony and ride that raggedy thing 'til the whistle blew. Hasn't stopped since. Mutton busting, barrel racing, saddle bronc, boy does it all. Not bad to look at while he does it, not that I'd ever admit it. It's probably my imagination, but seems like we've been trading looks here and there since the start of the year. Not that I'd ever admit *that*, either.

Ale and Tina swap glances with Markus and Zeke. Zeke fumbles the ball and pretends he wasn't looking. Devontae catches my eye.

"What's new, Hot Wheels?" he calls.

Hot Wheels. I was the one who gave myself that nickname back in second grade when I started following the WCMXers—they all give themselves high-flying names like that, and I wanted to be just like them. But Devontae's never going to let me live down that time in third grade when I drove over his toes on the playground. Wasn't my fault he and his buddies kept bulldozing right through our games—how else was I going to teach him some respect?

"You know how it goes, Boots." I shrug. "Breaking toes all over the county. Hearts, too."

Devontae's laugh got lower, deep and smooth like Karo syrup. "Wouldn't doubt it."

The bell rings, and we scatter to afternoon classes. Today I have art last period in one of the portables—single-wide trailers converted into classrooms, out behind the main building and connected by wooden walkways. They had a few at the elementary, too, but I never had classes in them. Here at the junior high, you get to them through an open courtyard that's broiling-hot when school starts in August and downright chilly come December.

The art portable has a long ramp with a tight 180-turn halfway up—a little tricky in the middle of a busy class change, but manageable. Like usual, I wait for the crowd to thin out first, then I get a fast rolling start and pop over the wooden lip at the bottom and onto the ramp.

Flying *down* ramps is more my thing, but scrambling up is a good challenge—all about finding that rhythm. Two hard shoves on my rims to get some speed, then grab the splintery wooden railings to keep it going. Shove, grab, yank. Shove, grab, yank. Like all untreated wooden railings in steamy-hot South Carolina, these leak gummy sap on sunny days, so my hands always end up sticky. I take a quick breather on the landing, work the 180, and start up the last half to the classroom door.

Then something shoves me from behind.

"I'll help you, Emmie!"

"I got it." I can't turn around without losing my rhythm, but I know that voice. It's Logan Whitten—jumpy as a frog and as tough to shake as a tick off a hound.

Logan's so eager to "help" he shoves my chair handles up, not down, which makes the front wheels dig in instead of pop up. The chair cuts sideways, bumping my still-sore elbow and digging a splinter into my palm.

"Logan!" I whisper sharply. "I'm good!" I can't let go of the railings to flick his hands away without losing ground, so I shove as fast as I can up the rest of the ramp.

We're getting looks from stragglers, probably wondering why I won't let him help me up the big bad ramp.

I don't like people messing with my chair, that's why.

The door to the art room is already shut, and Logan practically climbs over my chair to get to it. He bangs against my already loose handrim, and I'm about to wear him out over it, but then Devontae pushes open the door from the inside.

"May I do the honors?" he asks, bowing low like we're in some old-timey movie, and the angry words sort of melt from my mouth.

Now *that's* how you offer some help.

5

Room for Improvements

Other than the splinter in my hand, by the time art class ends, I've about brushed off the Logan ramp nonsense. Takes more than that to dent my junior-high thrill.

Seventh grade is the best. Changing classes, long, speed-worthy halls, getting to pick more classes and activities ourselves. More freedom = happy Emmie.

I'm catching a ride home with Ale's mom, so when the bell rings, I head to the gym to kill time while Ale checks out robotics club. After-school open gym is way cooler this year. Mr. Singletary, who's fresh out of teacher school and was a high school basketball legend right here in town, can finger-spin a ball forever and never flips out about a few tire marks on the wooden gym floor. I'm the first one there. Mr. Singletary tweets hello on his whistle as I go into the gym.

"Hey, Daredevil," he says, walking over and tossing me a ball. "Ready for some one-on-one?"

I'm not big on basketball, but one-on-one with Mr. Singletary is fun. Once everyone else starts playing, he and I battle it out under the lowest hoop—me on my wheels and him in his raggedy old, wheeled desk chair. A few other kids join the action using plastic floor scooters, and things get wild.

I dare Mr. Singletary to pop a wheelie, and he says he prefers his head unbusted.

"I'll leave stunts like that to the experts," he says, swiping the ball from my hands.

Dr. Grayling appears in the open doorway once and stands there, looking thoughtful, but doesn't come in. Then he goes away, and we all have fun until the after-after-school bell rings.

"Are we practicing tonight?" Ale asks as we wind home over the backroads.

"Not tonight." Since her mom's right there, I don't mention Dad's bedtime warning from yesterday.

"Want to do some collecting, then?" We fill orders about twice a week, but we can restock inventory any time the weather's good.

"I wish," I tell her with a groan. "It's supper at Nonny's tonight—have to do homework first. Tomorrow?"

Ale's abuela lives with her, teaches cumbia dancing

on Thursday nights at the community center, and is convinced the sun rises and sets on Ale and her siblings. Nonny can fill a whole mealtime with lists of things Dad and me could be doing better.

Unfortunately, the weekly dinner with Nonny and Pop-Pop—6 p.m., *sharp*—isn't up for debate. After Ale and her mom drop me off, I get straight on my homework and am done when Dad's truck pulls in.

At exactly 5:58, we drive between the two magnolia trees that mark the entrance to Valley View Mobile Estates. We pull into Nonny and Pop-Pop's driveway at 5:59 and are on our way inside at 6:01, past the perfect flower beds that line their little driveway. Their ramp is a bit shorter and steeper than the one Dad built at our place, so Dad gives me a boost from behind since we're running late.

"Wasn't sure you were coming" is how Nonny greets us. She looks at the clock.

"Wouldn't miss it." Dad's voice is the special sort of cheerful he uses on problem customers. "Smells good."

Nonny's eyes pin me like a butterfly as I pop over the threshold. "Emelyn, be careful!"

It wasn't even a big wheelie.

Dad's not the only one who's a bit different these days. Nonny wasn't ever what you'd call soft and fuzzy, but she wasn't quite this intense. Dad says it's because parents aren't supposed to have to bury their kids. He never says much about why he changed so much, too, but I guess everyone knows you're not supposed to bury your wife when you're just thirty-two. Especially not to some random, freak accident that nobody ever could've seen coming. Or planned for.

Sometimes I think it's too bad Dad and Nonny don't have wheels, too. Moving fast is the best way I know to keep ahead of feelings you'd rather shake off.

By the time dinner hits the table, I feel like a witness—or a suspect—in a crime show.

"You didn't wear *that* to school, did you?" Nonny looks at my raggedy jeans, purple Converse, and hearts-and-skulls hoodie like I scrounged them from the trash dump.

My mouth is full of mashed potatoes, so I take a long drink while I decide how to answer.

Dad breaks in. "How's the new hot water heater working?"

"Fine, if you like three-minute showers."

Dad spent an entire day picking it up and installing it for them. Also, there's no way the hot water lasts only three minutes. But that's gratitude, Nonny style.

Across the table, Pop-Pop gives me the blissful smile of someone whose hearing aids are totally still in the dresser drawer. "How's the business going, Biscuit?"

he asks, then hands me the plate of actual biscuits with a wink.

I dive into telling him about some of the coolest chair bags I've made lately, especially the Avengers one. I almost mention AK_SalmonGranny's cusswords-bag order but realize I probably shouldn't.

"I'm glad that sewing machine I gave your mother is getting use," Nonny says, slicing the sweet potato pie like it deserves punishment. "Have you tried the patterns I sent?"

Dad rescues me. "I'm not sure they're quite Emmie's style," he says, which is pretty tactful. Those dress patterns all looked straight out of some dinosaur decade.

"It wouldn't hurt for her to try a bit harder, Alan," she says.

Dad's face goes stony. "Emmie tries plenty." He stabs up his last bite of salad so hard his fork grinds against the bowl. "She's well on her way to earning herself some fancy new wheels."

Nonny can say more with a raised eyebrow than anyone else. "Priorities, Alan. A girl should look her best under the best of circumstances. In Emelyn's case, that's doubly important."

I know this conversation. Mom and Nonny used to squabble about it—Nonny arguing that a girl with a wheelchair should work extra hard on looking good in order to . . . what? Make the wheelchair turn invisible? Make strangers like me more? Mom, of course, biting back that I could wear a feed sack if I wanted to.

Someone squeezes my hand under the table. I glance at Dad, but his hands are shredding his napkin. It's Pop-Pop.

Dad's just about keeping it together. "Would you look at the time! Dinner was delicious, as always." He looks at me. "Emmie?"

I gulp down my last bite of biscuit and push away from the table so fast I almost pop an accidental wheelie. "Ready."

"You haven't had dessert—" Nonny protests, but Dad and I are out of there.

"Well, we've had worse," Dad says, when we're halfway home.

"If you say so."

"What do we always say? Shake it off . . ."

"And roll over it," I finish. It isn't Dad's fault Nonny does that. I know he'd like to tell her off as much as I sometimes want to. It's not that he doesn't love Nonny—we both do. I also sometimes feel like slipping Ex-Lax into her iced tea. Family is complicated.

It's only six forty-five when we get home. Dad has to study, so he spreads his books and manuals over the coffee table. It's still light out, and I'm dying to get back on that ramp and practice, but that's going to have to wait. I'm not sure exactly how serious Dad was about me staying off the ramp entirely, but right after a fun-filled dinner with Nonny is not the time to ask for clarification. The armrest should probably wait, too.

I tell him happy studying and head to my room to work on bags. I only have one new one—a medium-size armrest bag for a teenage guy down in Florida—and I message with Ale and Tina while I whip it up.

You going to make the AK lady one? Tina messages me.

Not sure yet, I write back.

This reminds me that I do need to answer AK_SalmonGranny's first message, or I'll look unprofessional. I send her a quick note that I'm a bit backed up and I'll get with her over the weekend to discuss her order. Then I fill Ale in about Dad telling me to stay off the ramp.

I knew it, she writes back. **Are we dead? We're dead, right?**

Not dead, I write back. **We just have to up our stealth factor.**

Maybe Dad got so squirrelly about me practicing jumps because he's worried what other people will think. When Mom died, Nonny wanted me to come and live with her and Pop-Pop. She wasn't the only one who thought a mechanic who liked to race dirt bikes wouldn't be the top pick to solo parent *a girl with Emmie's special needs*. Which is silly—Dad's been my wheelchair pit crew and all-around partner in mischief since forever. We take care of each other fine and—until recently—he never tried to stop me from taking a few chances now and then.

But working hard to earn new wheels is something I know Dad can get behind. Once I have that dream chair, he won't worry so much about me doing tricks and jumps. Back when he used to race himself, he kept his trail bike in perfect condition—he knows how much the right gear matters. Until then, maybe I can talk to Mr. Singletary about doing some practicing in the gym after school.

Right as I'm headed to bed, my computer pings with a new message from AK_SalmonGranny.

No rush, dear. We run on Alaska time up here. Look forward to employing your skills for the cause when you're available. You ever been king salmon fishing? —Dolly Mathisen

Her profile picture has changed from the fishing shot to one of her in some sort of off-the-wall parade with a bunch of other people. All of them are dressed up like in olden times, with floppy hats, over-the-top suits, and big dresses. Dolly's wearing fishnet stockings, a satin dress, and a red feather boa. Her wheelchair has a matching black boa and strings of shiny party beads.

Why can't I have a grandma like that? is my last thought before falling asleep.

The next morning, there's a plastic grocery bag hanging from the front porch railing with my name on it. It's full of neatly folded fabric pieces, with a note in Nonny's swirly, old-timey writing pinned to the top: *For your business.*

Family. It's complicated.

6

Sucky Ramps and Stinky Stealth

Maybe I've picked up some of AK_SalmonGranny's vibe, because the next couple days are just about perfect. Homework starts coming faster, but I stay right on top of it. Dad hits a balance between work and night classes and doesn't look as tired. The bag of fabric from Nonny turns out to have some cool vintage-looking prints.

On Wednesday, Mr. Singletary agrees to let me do some low-key chair tricks in the gym as long as he's there to spot me, and I spend a fun-filled hour popping over broom handles and through cones and working on a moving wheelie. Mr. Singletary is impressed, and I halfway convince him to let me try some easy tricks on the low stairs leading to the stage—which our gym has because it's also our auditorium. Dr. Grayling turns up in the doorway another time or two, but doesn't stay long.

In history class on Thursday, Mr. Milling makes half the class draw folded-up papers from an old Clemson helmet to pair us up for a semester-long project we're about to start, and when Devontae opens his and reads the name, he looks at me and winks.

Thursday after school, I wrap a bunch of change Dad's been tossing into a five-gallon water jug for ages. Our running deal is that he puts it in, I wrap it up, and we split the proceeds fifty-fifty. This time, my cut is enough to bump the red in my wall goal thermometer close to the 35 percent mark, and we celebrate with late-night sundaes at our favorite corner table at McDonald's.

On Friday afternoon, Ms. Hernandez catches up with me.

"Emmie!" She waves and hurries across the cafeteria, her heels clicking on the tile floor.

"Uh-oh," Ale whispers. "Want me to have an asthma attack?"

I'm half tempted, but then Ms. Hernandez slides onto the bench across from me.

"You have sixth-hour study period, yes?"

There's no point denying it.

"Good. I want you to stop by my office."

When she's gone, I pretend-bonk my head against the lunch table. "Too late for that asthma attack, Ale?"

So, instead of going to study hall, I head to Ms. Hernandez's office, which is attached to the school resource room. A few kids and aides are working together at different tables.

"Hi, Emmie," someone whispers from a nearby table. It's Ms. Merle, who used to be my school aide way back in first grade but now works here at the junior high. She gives me a big smile. "You hanging out with us today?"

I shake my head. "Just passing through!" I whisper back, not wanting to interrupt their work. I wave at a few kids I know and then head into Ms. Hernandez's office.

She has my file open on her desk. "How's your dad?" she asks. "He hasn't called me back about your 504—you gave him the letter I sent home last week, right?"

The letter is still stashed in the clutter on my desk. "He's been swamped," I tell her. "The 504 should still be fine—he said you can send a copy home for him to sign." The letter was actually asking if he wanted a 504 meeting, but I know there's no need. A 504 is basically a list of accommodations the school gives me now that I don't need a full IEP or extra services at school.

Ms. Hernandez arches an eyebrow. She's been the

head of our district's special education program since I started kindergarten. She and my mom didn't quite agree when my parents decided I didn't need to stay on services after fourth grade. She's nice, though, and now she smiles as she hands over my file. My 504 plan is paper-clipped to the top.

"I'll do that," she says. "Everything still look good?"

I take the paper and scan the short list of "reasonable accommodations" the school keeps on file for me.

1. Emelyn will have extra time of up to 5 minutes in order to maneuver her manual wheelchair in between classrooms, cafeteria, and gym settings on every day on which she attends school, in order to maximize her ability to independently access her educational environment.

No problem there. If the hallways weren't crowded, I could probably get between classes faster than everyone else.

2. Emelyn will have classroom seating options which are an appropriate height to accommodate her manual wheelchair, as well as seating close to the door, to ensure optimal access to work surface and to enter/exit classes with minimal manual difficulty.

That one's sort of funny, because none of the school's splintery old desks are much like the slick, shiny ones you see in movies about fancy schools. The teachers do their best to find one my chair fits at, or I can always work at a table.

3. ~~Emelyn will be offered opportunities to practice ambulating during gym class, with assistance from staff as needed, in order to maximize her access to school-based mobility.~~

That was another skirmish Mom helped me win. Just because you *can* walk—a little, sometimes—doesn't mean it's necessarily the best way to get around. Or that you should be forced to practice it at school.

"It looks fine." I push the paper back across the desk.

Ms. Hernandez studies me. "You're sure you don't want to change your mind about the walking practice?"

"I'm sure."

As I'm leaving, Ms. Hernandez follows me to the door. "Do me a favor, Emmie?"

"Okay?"

"Try and keep the speed under control. Dr. Grayling expressed some safety concerns."

"Never said anything to me," I say, but I remember how he's been hovering at the gym door sometimes. How he insists on playing doorman for me in the morning.

Ms. Hernandez sighs. "He worries about liability. A lot."

I tell her okay and head back to study hall, but I know it's no big deal. Everyone at school knows I move fast. Same as lots of other kids.

Seventh hour is art again. Tina and Devontae have the same class, so we go up the ramp together. Since we're a little late and Tina always asks if I want help instead of assuming, I let her push my chair up.

Ms. Jackson raises her eyebrows when we pile in a few seconds after the bell, but the Emmie-Get-Out-of-Jail-Free card does the trick, and she just waves at Devontae to close the door. Teachers mostly assume anyone who comes in late with me was helping me with something, which can be a handy alibi.

I'm itching for the day to be over. Devontae and me are meeting in the library after school to brainstorm history project ideas, which makes me feel sort of fizzy and weird at the same time.

When the bell finally rings, I remember I have to ask Ms. Jackson something. So I squeeze through the stampede and the cramped, portable classroom to her desk, get my answer, and head for the door. Tina's waiting at the bottom of the ramp, and Devontae's perched on the railing, drumming those outrageous cowboy boots of his against the bottom rail and saying something to

Logan, who's standing beside the ramp. Kids are going to stampede *up* the ramp soon for after-school art club, so I need to hurry.

Who am I kidding? Kids get out of my way if I need them to.

Truth is, I stayed up late bingeing on WCMX videos last night and have been sitting in school all day. I need to let off some steam. I need a little speed.

So I fling myself onto that long, rickety ramp, fast as a rock from a slingshot.

My wheels *bumpbumpbump* over the wooden slats like a heartbeat.

When he sees me flying toward the turn, Devontae shades his eyes with one hand and smiles big. He jumps down from the railing, and the blistering afternoon sun flashes off his rodeo belt buckle into my eyes. Which makes me fumble the turn a little. As I work my handrims to slow my momentum enough to make the 180, my right front wheel hits the railing.

I could have recovered it. But then . . . that *doggone* Logan.

He sees what happened and flies over to "help." Throwing his books aside, he gallops up the ramp like a mule with a burr.

Everything happens in a second.

Logan storms up the ramp and grabs my chair like some action hero.

I cut my wheels hard to dodge him and bang into the left side of the railing.

The bent armrest I haven't told Dad about finally breaks.

I grab the railing, and my hand hits a puddle of that steamy-hot, nasty pine pitch that always leaks out on hot days.

I wipe out.

No biggie. I fall all the time when I'm practicing jumps. All kids fall.

At the playground. On a sports field. Over their own feet.

But I fell with my wheelchair.

Instant panic. Some kids shout and run for teachers. Some stop to stare.

Doggone Logan *still* keeps pulling on my chair, hopping like a frog on a griddle and making it impossible for me to get back up. Finally, I haul off and whack him behind the knees. He yelps, lets go.

Devontae appears on the other side of the railing. "Fool, give her some space!" he barks, yanking Logan down the ramp. "You got this, Em?"

This isn't the time to say how I feel about his belt

buckle. "I'm good." Tina and Zeke reach us and hold off the goggling hordes while I get right-side up and down the ramp, shaking my head at the silliness of it all.

"Anything for attention, huh?" Tina says jokingly as we head across the courtyard.

"You know me," I banter back. I'm fine—just annoyed I bit the dust in front of everyone while *not* doing a super-cool trick. If I ever catch Logan alone beside an open locker, he's toast.

"Happens to the best of us." Devontae shows us a raw spot on his palm from gripping the reins last time he tried to stay on an ornery bronc—then flips up his sleeve to reveal the big bruise where he landed. "We pay to play, right?"

What a good way to put it. "You ready to hit the library?" I ask, glad to let the dust settle on this one.

Then three teachers run out of the building, looking panicked.

Crap.

At least Ms. Parsons doesn't flip out like everyone else.

She's been the school nurse since the dawn of time and happens to be here today. Country schools like ours don't get a nurse every day, so it's best to get hurt on Tuesdays or Fridays. I'm not hurt, but I still ended up here.

"What nonsense were you pulling?" She sloshes some alcohol on my arm and scrubs it with gauze.

"Ouch!" I yelp. "That's way worse than falling."

Ms. Parsons slaps a big bandage over my wound and hands me a wet washcloth for the pine pitch on my hands. "Uh-huh. You want to tell me about whatever stunt made you kiss that ramp?"

She's not truly mad. My dad has kept her old, silver Park Avenue running since I was barely big enough to reach the hood. The second time he replaced her water pump, I got to help. The fourth time, I had my own set of sockets and could do almost the entire job myself.

"That ramp is a disgrace," I inform her.

Ms. Parsons shakes her head so hard her big hair bun wobbles. "Why they put some of your classes out in those raggedy portables, I'll never know." She sighs. "Your momma would have raised Cain ten ways to Sunday."

Yeah, Mom would have had kittens about those ramps. I can totally imagine how that meeting would have gone.

Now, Mrs. Ethrige, you know we want the best for Emelyn at our school.

Excellent. Then tell me why we've had to struggle

to get that child's chair through the damn front door of this precious school for the past five years.

Well, now, that's a tricky one, I'll admit. But you know older buildings don't technically have to comply with the ADA, and inspectors haven't dinged us on it yet. Automatic doors don't come cheap. But I'd say we've done a rather fine job with those ramps.

Fine? The pitch is too steep, the rails are full of splinters, and don't even get me started about those floorboards.

I miss Mom.

"It's okay," I tell Ms. Parsons. "The ramp sucks. It was a regular old fall, no biggie."

To prove my point, I pop a wheelie and hold it while we talk. It's an impressive-looking trick, but not hard once you find your balance point. There's no way the athletic tape Ms. Parsons used to patch my busted armrest will hold up long-term, though. I'll have to tell Dad tonight.

"Maybe so," she agrees, putting up the gauze and alcohol. "But your stealth stinks. I know you like flash— but if you're ramming around like a sprayed cockroach, at least don't get caught."

I love her for saying that.

Speaking of flash, she should talk to Devontae about that belt buckle of his.

"Got it." I give her a smart salute while keeping my front wheels in midair. "Stealth and secrecy. I probably should get going. Thanks!"

Ms. Parsons shakes her head and pulls a sheet of paper from her desk.

"Not so fast, Emmie. We need to do an incident report on this one."

My wheels crash back to the floor. "Oh, come *on*! You're joking, right?"

"Girl, do I look like a joker to you?"

7

Meetings of the Mindless

"Want to work on our costumes?" Ale asks as her auntie pulls into my driveway.

"Maybe tomorrow." I *need* to get onto the ramp and blow off some serious steam. Wish I had a picture of Logan Whitten—*and* Fish—to put at the bottom so I could drive over them a few dozen times.

"Text me later? Or if you need help with . . ."

We hang out after school pretty much every day, but I don't feel like being around anyone right now—even my best friend. "I'm good, thanks. Just need some alone time." Maybe she can catch up on her hives instead. You wouldn't think bees would be high-maintenance pets, but Ale's always got something in them that needs checking. Or fixing or changing—I don't exactly keep track of what.

I thank Aunt Rosaria for the ride, go inside, and keep

fuming as I change clothes and get a snack. I don't know what time Dad's getting home, but I don't even care about getting caught. First things first. I bury Ms. Parsons's athletic tape underneath about ten pounds of duct tape until my armrest doesn't dare wobble.

Then I strap on my pads, adjust my helmet, and spend the next forty-five minutes angrily reminding myself that falling is No. Big. Deal.

It's still light when Dad pulls in. He bypasses the garage and drives straight into the field before I can pretend I haven't been on the ramp.

I keep hauling myself and my wheels to the top for another go. Might as well get in trouble again and make it an end-to-end crappy day. I imagine what Dad might yell and how I'll answer. Might even feel good to yell back.

But Dad isn't yelling. He climbs out of the truck, elbows the door shut, and leans against the fender. From the top of the ramp, I look over to see if he's going to try and stop me. For a second, he looks like he's about to, but then the mad look sort of melts off his face. He sighs, gives me a little nod and a wave, like, *Go on, then.*

I shove myself down the ramp. This time I actually get it, sort of. I tip sideways, but only after I've landed. And slowly enough that I can catch myself with one arm.

Dad walks over and sticks out a hand.

I grab on, and he tugs me and the chair upright.

"Not bad."

That's Dad. King of the understatement.

"Am I in trouble?"

"Probably should be." Dad pulls some grass from my wheels and chews on his lip. "Don't make a habit of it, but I heard you didn't have the best day."

"You did?"

"School called. So, we've got a meeting next week?"

"It's so stupid, Dad." All the frustration I've been working off rushes back like a hurricane. "I wouldn't even have fallen if everyone had left me alone!"

"Okay." Dad's not mad. Not at me, anyway. "Come on. Got a rear differential needs some TLC. You can fill me in."

I follow him to the garage, he uses the air compressor to blow the dirt and grass from my wheels and frame, and I tell him the whole saga while we work on a hearse from the funeral home. I end by telling him about the "game-plan meeting" Dr. Grayling called.

Dad whistles. "That's a sticky one."

"You're telling me." I pull out a broken screw and throw it at the workbench. It bounces off and barely misses Dad, who's wheeling out from under the hearse on his back. He sets the lift way down low when I work with him, so he ends up doing a lot of work on the wheeled creeper that looks like a big flat skateboard.

"Watch it, killer!" he teases, and hands me back the screw.

"Sorry." I sigh, then toss the screw—gently—onto the workbench. "It's *ridiculous*."

"I know, Emms." Dad sits up on the creeper so we're eye to eye. "I wish I'd known your armrest was broken. Why didn't you tell me?"

How can I say I didn't tell him because he's been so busy and tired lately? Used to be I wouldn't have had to say anything, because Dad was always on top of keeping my wheels in perfect condition, no matter what I'd been up to.

"I don't know. It wasn't that bad." I show him, and he immediately pulls the armrest off, cuts away all the tape, and takes it to the vise.

"How's that?" he asks after he finishes and slides it back into place.

It's perfect, like everything Dad fixes. "It'll last until I have my new wheels," I tell him. "Then you'll have no hope of keeping me off that ramp."

Dad's super proud I'm saving for the new chair. He was twelve, too, when he started cutting grass and pitching hay to save up for a truck. On his sixteenth birthday, he paid cash for a little candy-red Nissan pickup. He still drives it, and it looks and runs like new.

Dad doesn't grin back. "The new wheels are going to be swell," he says slowly. "And you know I support you working for them."

"But?"

"*But* let's focus on getting through this meeting first," Dad says. "You haven't had a fall at school in years— you sure you weren't being a bit reckless?"

"No!" I burst out. Like he should talk—Mr. Former Speed Demon himself. I explain—again—how it all went down.

"Okay," he says when I finish talking. "Okay. We'll deal with it."

Mom always handled the school meetings. Dad was always pit crew—and fantastic at it—but more than happy to let Mom deal with appointments and meetings and anyplace where talking was key.

Meetings of the minds, Dad used to call them.

Meetings of the mindless, Mom used to call them.

"Don't worry, Emmie," Dad says, like he can read my thoughts. "I know your mom was always more of the avenger, but we'll handle it."

When we've fixed the differential and tidied the

shop, I feel a little better. Also, the way Dad didn't even try and stop me from going down the ramp when he came home today makes me think—deep down—he hasn't forgotten what I can do.

Later on, I snag the laptop and show Dad some new extras I've been drooling over for my chair, and we admire heavy-duty suspensions and vinyl-coated handrims over dinner. Then Dad sits at the kitchen table to study, and I go to my room to fill some new orders. I make three pretty standard chair bags—one insect-printed for EntymoGeek78, one orange-trimmed camo for WisconnyBckHntr, and one triangle-shaped arm-rest bag made of fake fur for LARPerGirl06.

When I've stacked the packaged orders by the door for Dad to mail tomorrow, I go back to my room and stare for a long time at AK_SalmonGranny's order for the pink plaid, embroidered cussword bag.

I think about Logan refusing to let go of my chair.

Ms. Hernandez hinting *again* that I should be working on walking in gym class.

Dr. Grayling in the gym doorway, watching me pop wheelies and work hops with a face like an annoyed lemon.

I roll to my sewing machine, thread the bobbin with bright pink thread, and embroider every single cussword

I know onto a scrap of black cloth. When I'm out of words, my letters have gone from crooked to almost perfect, and I feel a tiny bit better.

Think it's time to make an ugly plaid bag for a cuss-loving, fish-catching Alaska grandma.

8

A Big Fat Grenade

I wake up twenty minutes before my alarm on meeting day, feeling ready.

We've got this. We do.

I load up a playlist of WCMX videos to gear me up and let them play in the background while I hurry around my room getting ready for school. When I'm done braiding my hair and lacing up my favorite red sneakers, the soaring stunts, berserk crowds, and bone-shaking music have me feeling like a gladiator. For extra luck, I thread purple ribbons through my spokes to match the ones in my braid before I head outside to meet Dad at the truck.

"See you at four," Dad says when we get to school. "I'll bring my game face."

"You better," I joke. He unloads my wheels, and we fist-bump; then he heads to work, and I join Ale and Tina.

"You ready?" Ale asks as we go to our lockers.

"Totally." I pop a wheelie.

"I hope it goes good, Emmie," Tina says. I know she's thinking about her mom's stories from when she worked with Dr. Grayling before. But I'm not worried.

"Dad and I have done this like a hundred times. We'll be good."

We know this drill. When all's said and done, it's a legal guardian's decision about whether to put a kid on specialized services—which is what I *know* this meeting is about.

We'll go to the meeting, do the dance. Then Dad will politely turn down services and sign the forms to get everyone off my back for another year. We went over it again last night, and I reminded Dad of how assertive Mom sometimes had to be not to get steamrolled by good intentions.

After school, I have half an hour to kill before the meeting, so I meet Devontae in the library to get started on ideas for our project. We spend more time geeking out about stunts—rodeo for him, wheels for me—than brainstorming, but there'll be plenty of time for that. We leave the library at 3:50, each promising to gather more ideas over the weekend.

At 3:55 p.m., I'm waiting for Dad outside the front office. Demarion Taylor comes down the hall just as his mom pulls to the curb to pick him up. She stops to let down the ramp to their van, so I wrestle open one of the heavy glass doors while Demarion steers his power chair—which is bigger and heavier than mine—through.

"Thanks, Emmie," he says with a friendly nod.

I nod back. "Anytime." I don't know Demarion super well—he's a couple years ahead of me and way more into art than sports—but we've always had that small spark of solidarity that comes with having to battle the architecture around here now and again.

At 4:00 p.m., I'm fidgeting with my handrims and fighting the urge to spin a few circles.

Dad rushes in at 4:05.

"You're late," I tell him.

"I know." Dad sounds distracted. "I'm sorry. We ended up three technicians short today—two sick and one family emergency."

This is a family emergency, I want to tell him. But I hold back, and we go into Dr. Grayling's big office. He and Ms. Hernandez are already there, and Mr. Singletary. He waves as Dad moves a chair to make space for me at the round table by the windows.

Dr. Grayling leans back and props his fingers under his chin. "Thank you for coming, Mr. Ethrige," he says. "I feel confident we can all find a good solution to this matter."

"There's no *matter*," I point out. "I'm fine, the ramp's fine. My dad already fixed my chair."

Ms. Hernandez taps one of her heels against the floor. "Nurse Parsons did say Emmie wasn't hurt—"

Dr. Grayling frowns. "That's certainly fortunate. What about Logan Whitten? He says Emelyn hit him in the knees, when he was trying to help the child up after her fall."

My temper sparks. "He wasn't *helping*!" *I'm not a child, either.*

"He tells me he was helping you back into your wheelchair."

"He's half the reason I fell! And I can get into my chair myself." I look at Dad for help, but he's studying the framed diplomas over Dr. Grayling's desk.

Dr. Grayling shakes his head. "I'm sure it was embarrassing," he says. "Under normal circumstances, I couldn't condone aggression against a fellow student—especially one who acted under good intentions. However, I'm willing to overlook it this once, though I will expect you to apologize to Logan."

I bite my cheeks, hard. This is where Dad *needs* to jump in and say something, but he doesn't. I can almost hear him thinking: *Shake it off—don't tell him off.*

Mom would have leaped over the desk and stuck Dr. Grayling's head in the wastebasket.

Deep down, I know Dad's not a talker. I can't stick my principal's head in the wastebasket, and telling him off won't help. But offhand charm—which has always served me well—just might.

I take a deep breath. Force a smile. "Are you enjoying working here so far?" I ask.

Dr. Grayling looks surprised. "Well, I suppose so," he says. "There's work to be done, of course, issues to be addressed. But everyone's been nice."

"Glad to hear it," I say, encouraged. "Are you for Carolina or Clemson?"

It goes like this for a minute or two—I throw out a steady stream of questions to divert him from my fall, my wheels, or Logan's bony knees. I ask about things I notice around his office—diplomas from far-away schools; some small woven baskets on his desk; a framed, faded picture of a lady who turns out to be his late wife—and it seems to be working. Dr. Grayling's slowly getting distracted by my charm offensive. He seems relaxed, more approachable.

Then Ms. Hernandez speaks up.

"To be on the safe side," she says, shuffling slowly through my file with her perfect fingernails, "we might consider Emmie for re-entry into special education services."

Wait. No!

"That will help us determine where Emmie might benefit from additional supports," she continues, like she didn't just lob a big fat grenade into my perfect seventh-grade year.

Dr. Grayling snaps to attention. "Yes." He sets down the photo of his wife and swivels his chair away briskly. "Safest course of action for all concerned."

This is exactly where Mom would have leaped in, armed with printouts about disability rights and perfect responses to everything Dr. Grayling and Ms. Hernandez suggested.

I look desperately at Dad, my only remaining hope. He fidgets in his chair, swiveling side to side like sitting still is killing him. He's got circles under his eyes, dark and bruise-y, and he's still wearing a grease-smudged, button-up work shirt with his name embroidered on the chest.

I try not to think about the clean shirt I ironed and left on his bed last night.

"I—" Dad's gaze bounces from Dr. Grayling in his perfect suit to Ms. Hernandez's perfect nails tapping my file. At Mr. Singletary, looking uncertain across the table. He clears his throat. "I suppose it couldn't hurt to check things out again. To be on the safe side," he adds. He doesn't look at me. Lucky for him, because the laser eye beams I'm shooting would barbecue him into charcoal.

Before I can whip up more fake charm to stop this runaway bus, it's done. Decided. The situation is officially immune to my charms.

I sit there, stunned, as the adults work out the details around me. When it's all wrapped up, Dr. Grayling escorts us out—and then pushes my chair halfway down the hall. "Don't worry, Emelyn!" he says as he trundles me along like a shopping cart. "Sometimes we just need a little help to accept a little help."

Shake it off—don't tell him off.

Shake it off—don't tell him off.

I *really* want to tell him off.

9

Traitors Don't Get Sympathy

The first half of the ride home, I'm too shocked to say anything.

The second half, I'm too mad.

Dad's silence is so thick I can almost taste it. But his fingers fidget on the steering wheel, so hard he even beeps the horn by mistake.

I study the patchwork of soybean and cotton fields and the pine trees as they pass by my window. If he's waiting for me to say something, tough.

"Emmie—" he finally tries as we turn onto our road.

"I'm *fine*."

I'm obviously *not* fine, but Dad doesn't push it. The second I'm out of the truck, I roll straight for the paved path that winds through the scrubby woods from our place to the edge of Ale's driveway. I get all the way there before I remember it's Friday and almost crash into Ale when she walks out of the shed, geared up in her bee suit and veil and carrying a lit hive smoker thingy. Ale always does her hive checks on Fridays.

"Emmie, hey!" She shifts the smoker so it won't blow in my face. "How was the . . . ?" she starts to ask, then trails off. "That bad, huh?"

"Worse."

"I'm doing hive checks, but how about we talk when I get them closed back up?"

I wish she'd leave the silly bees and come talk, but Ale always says you shouldn't open and close a hive too many times. "How about we talk while I help check hives?"

That gets Ale's attention. "Wow, that must have been some meeting."

I'm scared enough of Ale's bees that hive-check day usually makes me avoid her place like toxic waste. It's bad enough that her hives are in a small clearing right behind the Ches' shed (instead of buried some-place far, far in the woods). But today I'm so steamed, I swallow my fear and put on Ale's spare bee suit and veil. Then I hold wax-filled frames for her while she inspects bees on them with a big magnifying glass like a bug-loving Nancy Drew. Holding a million buzzing bees on my lap is terrifying enough to water down my anger a bit—their noise is even oddly soothing today.

Still, I pray they won't all decide I'm an enemy while I tell Ale about the disastrous meeting.

"Dang," she says, looking up from the honeycombs where she's been searching for the queen bee. "Your dad didn't say anything?"

"No!" I feel hot all over, remembering how Dad just sat there. Let the whole meeting happen around him and signed off on whatever they wanted. Mom would have gone feral.

"What now?" Ale asks, running a soft brush gently along the edge of the frame.

"Not sure." I try to ignore the three bees marching over my veil—about two inches from my face. "Usual hoops, I guess. Maybe have to see the PT to prove I can get around school fine. Ms. Hernandez wants me to go back on special ed services."

"Didn't you finish all that like three years ago?" Ale frowns.

"Yeah. And the school hasn't even been able to find a full-time PT in over a year." I make a fist, then remember the frame full of pointy-ended insects I'm holding. "Fish even said something about an aide." That part, at least, I'm not quite as worried about. I know most of the aides at school already, and they stay super busy with the kids who do need extra help during the day. That should work in my favor until I can figure a way out of this mess.

Like my mom always used to say, *Strong voice, calm voice. That's how you get folks to listen.* Charm and speed have always been more my thing, but I may have to pull out some of Mom's tools, too. Then I giggle, remembering how often Mom's "calm voice" would boil over into something pretty fiery.

"I bet you could talk to your dad." Ale bends over the frame with the magnifying glass again. "He's not exactly the original rule follower, is he?"

It's true. My dad was never big on silly rules, which makes all this more frustrating.

"There she is!" Ale says suddenly. "Her Royal Highness." I follow her pointing finger to the queen bee, bigger than the rest, with a cluster of other bees surrounding her like flower petals. I admit I don't always pay close attention when Ale goes on about her bees, but I know the queen is the boss of the whole hive.

Wish I was a queen bee. Then everyone would have to listen to me.

By Monday morning, I'm almost glad to get back to school. The silence around our place has been thick as pluff mud. Dad took off for the shop the second we got home and hasn't stopped moving since. I spent most of Saturday at Ale's and Sunday perfecting one-word answers. Not that Dad said much that needed answering.

Dad has to be at work early today, so he drops me at school thirty minutes early. I don't mind a bit. I still feel hot as a teakettle about to whistle.

"We'll work this out, Emmie." Dad puts my lunch in my lap and tries not to yawn. "Things'll let up a bit after this week, and then let's talk."

He's got dark circles under his eyes again, but I remind myself he's a traitor, and traitors get no sympathy. "Whatever," I tell him. "Late night tonight?"

He nods tiredly and pulls my wheels from the bed, and we say goodbye.

Inside, the mostly empty hallways are a welcome sight. Even though it's been a week since my wipeout, I still feel like there's a hundred more eyes on me than usual. But not in the good *Hey, Emmie, did you catch the game/let's grab lunch/you going out for drama club on Friday?* kind of way. Now it's more like everybody's wondering if I'm going to break or randomly topple over.

I head toward my locker and am surprised by Devontae leaning against the wall, one cowboy boot propped up, flipping through a horse magazine. He looks over when he hears me coming.

"Hot Wheels." He grins over the magazine and nods at the red-and-black armrest bag with silver trim I made last night. "I like the new saddlebags."

"Thanks. You already getting ready for 4-H?" I nod at his magazine. Devontae always goes in for 4-H, usually horse judging or hippology or something like that. He even got his own horse last year. I dig through my locker and wonder what Devontae is doing hanging out in this hallway when his locker's way down around the corner.

"I wrote down a few ideas over the weekend," he says. "Want to trade lists?"

Crap. The project. "Maybe a little later, okay? Still working on mine."

I don't mention that I haven't exactly started yet, but Devontae says sure and falls into step beside me as I head back down the hallway. It's still early, and Devontae pauses at the gym door. "Want to shoot a few baskets?"

Mr. Singletary lets anyone play ball before the morning bell, so Devontae asking this isn't any big thing. But I get a tiny bubbly feeling that's a nice change from the angry-teakettle one I've been choking on all weekend.

Then a voice calls, "Emelyn Ethrige?"

Standing outside the front office is a lady with a dyed-blond ponytail. She's too old to be a student, but she's dressed in a pink-camo sweatshirt and jeans, so probably not a teacher. She looks lost.

"You know her?" I whisper to Devontae.

He shrugs. "Someone's mom?"

The lady looks at a paper in her hand and back to me. At my wheelchair. She walks over. "You're Emelyn, right, sweetie?"

She talks like every word is something to get excited over. A bit loud, like she's not sure I understand. I hate being called *sweetie* almost as much as when people grab my chair, so being polite takes effort.

"Emmie, yeah. Do you need directions?" The building is a little confusing.

"Aren't you sweet!" The lady sticks the paper in her sweatshirt pocket, and I see a little butterfly tattoo on her wrist. "No, sweetie, I don't need directions. I found you right here!"

"What's she talking about?" Devontae whispers. I try and remember if I've had any local shop orders lately—but even if I had, I'd never have someone meet me at school.

"I'm so excited to be here," the lady says. I can't imagine what could be exciting about old E. L.

Pinckney at 7:45 a.m., but adults are strange some-times. "Dr. Grayling even did a special rush hire for me," she adds. "Said it was urgent."

Then I get it. *Oh, no.*

No, no, no.

"Sorry, wrong Emmie!" I grab Devontae's arm and spin my chair around. "Come on—we playing ball or what?"

Devontae looks from the lady to me. "But, who—"

"*C'mon!*" I hiss. But it's too late. The lady looks, if possible, even more excited.

"I'm your new educational aide!"

This isn't happening.

"We have all day to start getting to know each other!"

I suddenly, desperately, wish for a supercharger strong enough to launch my wheels—and me—through the front door. Or the wall. Or anywhere but here.

"It'll be so much *fun!*"

Not even 8 a.m., and I've already heard the biggest joke of my whole day.

10

We All Fall Down

FROM: Tatiana Hernandez, EdM, Office of Exceptional Children
TO: Alan Ethrige
RE: Emelyn Ethrige's Individualized Education Plan (IEP)

Dear Mr. Ethrige:

I am writing to recap our very productive team meeting regarding Emelyn's emergent needs at school. As we all know, Emelyn is well known to the Barndale County School District 3 family as a dynamic, determined, and energetic girl and has long inspired the entire community.

New school years can bring new barriers and may require different programming for our special students. Emelyn's recent fall, even with adaptive architecture in place, as well as acting out toward a fellow student, has flagged a team recommendation to consider additional supports at this time. Based upon our team meeting, the following adjustments to Emelyn's individual student plan are proposed:

1. Emelyn will be evaluated for potential reentry into the BCSD3 Program for Exceptional Needs, to assess further need for supports such as physical therapy, safety-awareness training, etc.
2. Emelyn will refrain from risky behavior while negotiating school-based settings and architecture (unnecessary wheelies, excessive speed in hallways, reckless behavior on ramps, etc.), in order to minimize risk to herself or others.
3. Emelyn will be assigned a one-on-one aide at school, in order to ensure her personal safety, assist her with physical tasks as needed, and offer strategies to help Emelyn find appropriate methods for expressing frustration.

Please do not hesitate to contact me with any questions about these proposals. We the team feel confident that, with the appropriate assistance and guidance, Emelyn will have a successful year!

Go Swamp Foxes!
Sincerely,

Tatiana Hernandez
Tatiana Hernandez, EdM
Program Coordinator, Office of Exceptional Children

Dr. Bruce Grayling
Dr. Bruce Grayling, MA, EdD
Principal

11

A Big Fat
Train Wreck

I can't believe this.

Our county's one of the poorest in the state. Teachers buy their own printer paper and art supplies. Heck, our school has a few toilets that've been busted so long the janitors could just plant flowers in them and call it a day.

But less than seventy-two hours after that meeting they've managed to hire an official, full-time Emmie Sitter.

By the time she checks in at the office and gets a copy of my daily schedule from the secretary, I can tell this lady—Dawn Wanamaker—is a first-time aide. "Okay. So . . . where's your first class?" She sounds suddenly nervous, like I might ask her to carry me there on her back.

The first bell rings, and kids flood the hall. Devontae

says something else, but I plunge into the crowd—his first class is the opposite way, anyhow. Dawn trails after me as I plow toward first period, her half trying to push my chair and me half dragging her along. I stop quick outside my first class, and she bumps into me.

"I push my own chair." We need to get a few things straight.

Dawn blinks her violet-shadowed eyes. "Oh! Okay. At the interview, they said I should be prepared to help with anything you needed!"

I'll bet. I picture Principal Fish head-down in a trash can. "And my ears work fine."

More blinks and a scrunched-up forehead.

"You're talking super loud. And slow." In case that's not clear enough, I add, "My *legs* aren't up to code. Ears are A-okay."

"I . . . oh. Right. Sorry." Dawn's cheeks get red, and she stammers a bit, but then the last bell rings and I scoot into class, leaving her to follow.

By midmorning, I'm ready to throttle Dawn.

If the almost baby voice—which, okay, she does quiet down—wasn't enough, I suspect everything she knows about wheelchairs comes straight from bad movies. Instead of sitting at the back of the classroom, like a sensible person, she drags a chair right to my desk. Subtle.

She randomly leans on my chair.

She touches my armrest bag without asking.

She asks *so many* questions.

"So, what happened to you, honey? Car accident?"

"You can get your lunch by yourself? That's wonderful!"

She's trying so hard, but being around her vibe feels like drowning in glitter and rainbow sprinkles. Shiny and sweet and not exactly real.

I grind my teeth and roll faster.

"I had to use crutches once. Broke my ankle falling out of a tree stand—so much for *that* deer season! So, I *get* what it's like. Don't know how you do it all the time—I sure couldn't!"

Like I've never heard *that* one before.

"Careful, honey! Not too fast!"

I cope as best I can. I mentally shake her voice away, like sparkles in a snow globe. I pay perfect attention to my teachers. I answer Ale's and Tina's silent *What the heck?* looks between classes with a whispered "Tell you later" and then beat it to my next class with my new pink-camo shadow trailing me, trying to check her phone without being obvious and aggressively attempting to connect with me.

By midafternoon, I've worked out a rough plan. All day, I've been secretly writing down the ways Dawn's tried to give me help I don't need. Once I show Dad, he'll see how over-the-top this has gotten, and we'll schedule another meeting with Ms. Hernandez to let her know the aide thing isn't going to work out.

Until then, I know Dad wouldn't want me to make the aide feel bad. *She's just trying to do her job, Emms*, I can practically hear him say. Honestly, Mom would have said it, too.

Besides, annoying or not, Dawn *is* a grown-up, and I wasn't raised in a barn.

So I try not to show how frustrated I am.

Then she follows me right into the bathroom.

When I hiss at her that I'm fine, she can stand outside and play on her phone until I'm done, she asks a few more mortifying questions first. Loudly. In the middle of the crowded hallway.

While Zeke and Devontae happen to be walking by.

That does it. I hide in the bathroom a few minutes to get it together. I cuss at the sink, the toilet, and the mop bucket. This has to stop. When I bash my way back out through the door, making Dawn jump, I don't much care about being polite anymore. By the time the end-of-day bell rings, Dawn looks as ready to escape as me.

"So, today was . . . fun!" she tries.

"Uh-huh." I don't think anyone's fooled.

She beats it out the front door, and I take off to find

Ale. She and Tina are already looking for me. I spill the details of my train wreck of a day—chair grabbing, bathroom following, and every awful moment between. Except the part about Devontae getting a front-row view of both cringe-worthy moments, because that's too awful to mention.

Tina groans when I finish. "I told you Dr. Grayling was going to be trouble," she says. "My mom said he was like this over in Harper Three, too. *Well intentioned, but a real stickler*, she said. He even decided kids couldn't flip on the jungle gym without an adult spotting them!"

Ale scowls a minute, then grins. "Well, what shall we do about it?"

"I tell my dad," I say. "Then we talk to Ms. Hernandez again." I try to remember which evenings Dad will be home this week.

Ale's grin widens. "Then, mi querida," she says slowly, "until then, we'll have to give your new shadow some on-the-job training, won't we?"

12

Double Down

Ale's words stick with me the whole ride home. Deep down we both know making Dawn's job harder isn't the nicest thing to do, but I can't help daydreaming about it—just a little.

"Think it over," Ale says, whispering so her mom won't hear us. "A little creative mayhem might help."

"Let me talk to Dad first," I tell her. "We might not even have to."

After Ale's mom drops me off, I go inside, log on, and check my shop. I tally last week's sales and double-check tracking on in-transit orders. The only bag that hasn't arrived is the one for AK_SalmonGranny. I guess mail's a little slow out on some wild Alaska island.

A text from Ale chimes in. **Operation Mayhem, chica. Say the word and we'll have that aide itching for a job at the library.**

Ale always knows how to cheer me up, but I'm still betting on getting Dad on my side. I look at Salmon

Granny's amazing profile again and wonder if anyone ever gives her crap about what she can and can't do. She doesn't seem like someone who would care—or even listen—but who knows if she's anything like her profile in real life?

Wish I had an alter ego sometimes. But it's hard to invent one when you've lived the same place your whole life, and everybody knows you down to the bone.

I've got three new customer reviews—five stars. The best one is from NotYourPrairiePrincess04.

Purchased from HalfpipeEmms on August 25

Armrest bag, small with ribbon ties

This was my first order from Emmie but not the last! My new bag fits perfectly over my armrest, doesn't get tangled in my spokes or get in the way. Plus, AVENGERS???!!! My mom took my brother and me to Fargo last week for school shopping and TWO random people came up to me—and not to ask what happened to me! One was wearing Iron Man earrings and one had a Captain America hat. They just wanted to geek out over my bag. ☺ Thanks a million, Emmie.

Best. Review. Ever.

When I've added up my earnings, I color in my wall chart up to the $2,025 mark. Progress is slow, but steady. I think about Prairie Princess (her real name is Jewel) again and how my simple little bag started up a conversation with two strangers that wasn't about her wheels. I totally get how cool it is when that happens.

I wonder if she has to have an aide at school.

Thinking about that buries my slightly happier mood like sand on a campfire. It's hard to explain why I'm so mad without sounding like a jerk. I *know* aides are important—and some kids really need them at school. Like Demarion, whose arms and legs are paralyzed. Or Rodney, who had a bad head injury three years ago. Or Kimmy or Lavardis or Rhianna—or plenty of other kids.

I needed one, too, when I was little. But now I *can* do just about everything for myself—I have for years. All I need these days are my wheels and for people to not get in my way.

A better ramp or more accessible bathrooms at school wouldn't hurt, either.

I look down at my new armrest bag Devontae noticed this morning. Before the day went south, I felt tingly all over when I saw him waiting near my locker. I untie the bag, flip it over, and read the secret, salty words I sewed on the back in silver thread. Words more deep-down honest than I could ever say. I hope AK_SalmonGranny likes her sassy new bag, too.

After working on orders a little longer, I do a good enough job on my homework and then switch back to WCMX videos while I make dinner and rehearse the

Very Mature Speech I'll give Dad when he gets home, so we can head back to school and sort this all out ASAP.

I hear Dad's truck pull in around seven, but he goes straight to the shop instead of coming inside, which means he's got a job to finish. So I spend another hour designing more bags—simple, straightforward patterns with basic trim. I make them reversible, and on one side of each one I embroider a saying. I don't use any cusswords this time, but every bag I make tonight gets a tiny dose of sass.

Hands off the chair, please.

Ears work great, thanks.

Ask me my order, not them.

When I'm done, I post pictures, make new listings, and put the bags up for sale. I feel a little nervous, like I'm doing something I shouldn't—even though everything I wrote on them is just plain truth.

Dad drags his tail inside around eight thirty, looking exhausted. "No worries," I tell him, before he can apologize. "I saved some dinner." I get busy fixing a plate, mentally rehearsing everything I'm going to tell him about Dawn.

But Dad doesn't want the BLT and tomato soup I give him. He flops into his chair, flips on the television, and then flips it right back off.

"How was school?" he asks.

I'm not fooled by his attempts to act chill. I may still be annoyed with him, but I know when something's off.

I look at him, eyebrows up, until he caves.

"Failed my test," he admits. "Crash and burn."

Oh man. "That stinks." I know how hard he studied.

I go over and punch him on the arm. "You'll get the next one, right?"

My pep talk doesn't pep Dad up. He shakes his head, looking dazed. "Don't know what happened. It was like I hadn't studied a bit. Could've been in Klingon."

Dad looks so miserable—drastic action is clearly needed. I whip around the kitchen and create two root beer floats topped with rainbow sprinkles and hot cocoa powder. I throw some cinnamon and nutmeg on, add a bit of pepper for good measure, and bring him one. Dad manages a tiny grin.

"Your mom would be proud." He sips it and makes a thinking face. "Not bad."

When I was tiny, I'd help Mom cook, and she'd let me figure out what tasted good by putting out all the spice bottles and letting me choose which ones we'd have on our dinner. This meant we'd sometimes have chicken with nutmeg and tapioca . . . or milkshakes with pepper. Dad and Mom were good sports about eating whatever random combos I came up with.

This float is pretty good, even with the pepper, and I'm glad it made Dad smile. This is when I should tell him about Dawn. He might even find it funny—in a twisted way—and I know he'd see my point.

Then I see he's already half dozed off right there in his chair. Those little squint lines around his eyes look sharper in the TV's glow. I hesitate, my hand halfway out to poke his arm.

I sigh and shift gears. Instead of shaking Dad awake, I get a blanket from the sofa—the soft, purple one that was Mom's favorite—and cover him up. I get his phone from the coffee table, make sure the alarm's set, and turn off the TV. As much as I'm dying to shake my new shadow, tonight's not the best night to tell Dad about Dawn. He's got enough to worry about right now.

I'll have to double down on dealing with her myself for now. Piece of cake, right?

13

Glue Your
Mouth Shut

The next morning, I'm waiting for Dawn when she arrives.

"Hi, Dawn!" I chirp. "Ready for more fun?"

Dawn looks confused—then her beauty pageant smile blinks on. She pockets her phone.

"You got it, girl!" she chirps back, sounding mostly eager and a tiny bit wary.

She pulls off her pink-camo cap and stashes it in her bag, and I make cheerful, pointless conversation all the way to homeroom. Second period, I smile like a bobblehead as she peeks at my quiz to see if I need help filling in answers.

When she squeals over my fall-themed bag, I untie it and hand it over for a closer look. She pauses over what's stitched on the back but hands it back without saying anything.

She's thrown at first by my sudden cheerful chattiness. By about fourth period, she's chatting back—about her family, scrapbooking, and her miniature Doberman, Scooter. I listen, wide-eyed, saying *uh-huh*, *wow*, and *so cool*! As if scrapbooking doesn't sound like a total snooze.

In the lunchroom, I let Dawn get my tray and carry it to where Ale and Tina are sitting. They look at me strangely.

I give them a *Hold that thought* look.

Later, when Dawn gets up to refill my drink, I lean over the table toward Ale.

"All systems go," I whisper. Her eyes light up.

"When do we start?" she whispers back.

Then Dawn comes back with my drink. "Shoot!" I say loudly. "Left my Spanish book in my locker."

Ale and Tina manage to keep straight faces. Dawn snaps up the bait like a largemouth on a worm. "I'll get it, sweetie!" Then she pauses. "Will you be okay a sec without me?"

Ale cuts in smoothly. "We'll be here if Emmie needs anything. Don't worry!" She darts her eyes my way, and I look away fast so I don't start laughing.

I scribble my locker combo on a napkin and hand it over. "Thanks a bunch!"

"My pleasure!" Dawn practically skips across the lunchroom and out the courtyard door.

I stuff some grapes into my mouth and wonder if I look as smug as I feel.

Tina and Ale start snickering. We all know I don't have Spanish today.

It's not like we spend the *whole* week messing with Dawn. I mean, there's class and homework and finishing last-minute costume touches for the Fairy Festival on Sunday. I also spend some effort avoiding the guys—well, Devontae, mostly, telling myself it's because I still haven't made my idea list for our project. Not because it's dead embarrassing having Dawn tail me like a bird dog. Even though it's both.

But every day, I send Dawn on some roundabout errand to find something I "forgot" or to deliver an urgent message to one of my teachers. I even have her convinced I can't tie my own sneakers, so she gets right down and knots them for me as soon as I come in every morning. On Thursday, she gets me an extra Jell-O after I tell her soft foods are easier for me to digest.

Childish, maybe, but at least acts of mild mayhem are something I can control. Also, since most everyone's in on the joke, it shifts the embarrassment factor off me. A little.

It doesn't last. On Friday, Ms. Hernandez snags me on my way to study hall.

"Okay, Emmie," she says. "My office. Eat a bunch of caramels, shall we?"

Eat a bunch of caramels is Ms. Hernandez's way of saying, *You're in trouble, ma'am, but you can raid my candy bowl while I decide your fate.* Think she got it from some old movie.

Oh well. I'm a little hungry, anyway.

Dawn starts to follow us, but Ms. Hernandez waves a handful of perfectly polished nails.

"You can take a break, Ms. Wanamaker. Meet us at my office in fifteen minutes."

Dawn happily heads toward the courtyard, phone out, and I follow Ms. Hernandez to her office. She sets the candy bowl on her desk and gives me a sharp look.

"Okay," she says. "How about you tell me what's going on?"

I shovel four caramels into my mouth so my answer will be extra sticky.

"You know," I mumble. "Classes, good. Friends, good. Took up sewing over the summer. I'll have to show you the fairy costume I'm making."

Ms. Hernandez isn't distracted. "That's fascinating,

but not what I mean. What have you been doing to Ms. Wanamaker?"

Two years ago, my best wide-eyed look would have made Ms. Hernandez wave me out of her office with a head shake and a half-hidden smile. Now she seems to expect a bit more.

"Okay, fine." I relent. "I *may* have given her some errands to do. You know, so she feels useful. Everyone likes that, right?"

Ms. Hernandez looks at me over her trendy orange glasses and sighs. "Have another caramel," she says. "Emmie," she adds, "I get how you feel about having an aide."

"Doubt it." The words slip out on me.

"That's a little rude, don't you think?"

No. Just true. I quickly glue my mouth up with two more caramels, but Ms. Hernandez patiently outwaits me, nails tapping, until I give up and swallow.

"Other kids fall sometimes," I point out. "So why don't you suggest *they* all get aides?"

Ms. Hernandez looks a little uncomfortable, but then a student comes in with an urgent message from the office. Ms. Hernandez, clearly grateful for the escape, tells me to try harder to get along and that I can wait here for Ms. Wanamaker. Then she's out of there.

Seemed like a fair question to me.

Ten seconds after she leaves, I'm hightailing it down the hall. It's only been seven minutes, and Dawn's nowhere in sight. *Freedom.*

I roll hard through the empty hallways until I'm at the library wing. My study hall is in the other direction, but the quiet library is just what I need right now, so I roll in, planning to check out the graphic-novels shelf. Then I turn down a row and almost run smack over Devontae, who's sitting on the floor reading a book. He yanks his legs back just in time.

"Long time no see." He closes the book over his thumb to keep his place. "Been hiding somewhere?"

"Not exactly. Hope I didn't scuff the boots." I start to pass him, but he stops me.

"You've sort of taken off in the other direction every time you've seen me this week. Do I need to switch deodorants, or was it something I said?"

"Deodorant. Didn't want to come out and say it." I smile to let him know I'm joking.

Devontae's still seated, putting him right below eye level. Looking down to talk to someone doesn't happen to me often. Tougher to avoid his eyes this way. "We're cool," I add.

"Good," he says. "Then we should probably get moving on that project. You had any time to brainstorm?"

He looks about to say more, and I hope he's not going

to ask about Dawn. There's no good way to explain it. She's probably hunting for me now—I half expect the loudspeaker to blast my name any second. I make myself look at him. "A bit, yeah," I hedge. "Should be ready to trade lists soon." Somehow, I'll figure out how to do that without Dawn.

"Cool. You busy this weekend?"

The question throws me. Does he want to get together for our project? "I've got the Fairy Festival with Ale and Tina on Sunday. You?"

"I'm riding in the Setzler Junior Open on Saturday."

Setzler's is the local rodeo arena, over on Horse-feathers Road.

"If you're not busy, you want to come watch? I can get you a free ticket. It'll be a good show, especially if I get bucked off." He grins, like he's sure he won't get bucked off.

It takes me a second to realize he's not talking about getting together for our project. I feel a grin about to bust loose, but then my brain starts racing when I remember the setup at Setzler's. The soft, sandy field. The tiny, cramped porta-potties with the big step up.

"I can't," I blurt, more bluntly than I meant to.

Devontae's face falls. "Oh," he says.

Shoot. That didn't come out right. "I mean, rodeo's cool and all, it's not—"

Devontae's on his feet before I can finish.

"Don't sweat it," he says in a buttoned-down voice. "Forget I asked. Maybe next week for the project, then?"

He ducks around me and makes tracks out of the library. His book—a biography of someone named Bill Pickett—lies forgotten on the floor beside my right front wheel.

Well, crap.

Should've swiped a few more caramels from Ms. Hernandez's bowl. That all would've gone down a whole lot better if I'd glued my mouth shut first.

14

Look Around You!

"Sure you don't want to stay home?" I ask Dad on the morning of the Fairy Festival. He could probably use the time to study for his class.

Dad shakes his head. "And miss my yearly chance for weird-watching?"

I half turn to punch him, and he laughs. "Just kidding. You look wonderful, Emms." He finishes zip-tying the stuffed parrot to my chair back and stands up. "There you go."

"Perfect." My pirate fairy theme really came together, and I know I look good in my red-white-and-black-striped costume, especially the dozens of shredded ribbons sewn to my sleeves. I've threaded black and silver ribbons into my spokes and hung a little Jolly Roger down the back of my chair.

I adjust a loose ribbon and realize Dad's looking at me funny. "I forget an earring?" I reach up to check the little dangling skulls.

"What? No." Dad shakes his head like he's clearing cobwebs. "You . . . look a lot like your mom right now."

I remember Mom's old costumes, hanging in the bedroom closet that's all Dad's now. It's no secret where I got my love of dressing up. Dad looks about to say something else but then quickly goes to the fridge to get some water bottles to bring. Then we go pick up Ale and Tina.

Tina's got a dark fairy vibe, black dress and fingernails and tiny silver wings. Ale's bee fairy costume looks incredible—she's added yellow tulle to the skirt to make it extra full and has tights with a gold honeycomb pattern and delicate gold antennae. We admire each other's looks and pick on Dad's sorry old chainsaw chaps, but when we get there and park in the big hayfield that's doubling as a parking area, he surprises us by pulling a brown-and-green tunic thing from a bag stashed behind his seat.

"You're not the only one who shops online," he says, laughing at my surprise as he pulls it on.

The festival grounds are in the woods, down a long hill from the parking field. As we step into the shade of the trees, the temperature drops, and the colored ribbons shivering in the trees above us make everything feel magical. Must have rained recently, because the steep, narrow path is full of thick, red-clay mud that the sun hasn't quite reached. It quickly starts bogging down my wheels. Dad and I are used to this, so he scoops me up, leaving Ale and Tina to fold my chair and carry it down.

"I don't know, Emms," he jokes as he steps carefully through the mud and the rest of the costumed crowd. "You better not grow any more, or your old dad might keel over." When we get down the hill and clear of the mud, I reclaim my wheels, and we head through the entrance arch.

The Fairy Festival is like a ren faire, a comic con, and a music fest mashed into one. People pretty much wear whatever they want, with a loose fairy-ish/medieval theme, and spend the day pretending they're in a different world than this one. We mingle with pirates and fairies, goblins and trolls, performers walking on sky-high stilts, and people dressed as woodland sprites hiding along paths and peering at us through colored crystals held up to their eyes. Once he's satisfied the paths down here are dry enough not to sink my chair and there's a bathroom I can get into, Dad ducks off on his own, reminding us to meet him at the music stage in two hours.

We barely slow down all morning, watching performers, getting into character, and poking through the pop-up shops that are full of weird, wonderful things. Trinkets and treasures and unbelievable costumes. Ale and I even get a few ideas for things we could make to add to our own shop.

"Check that out," Tina says, looking at a guy a little older than us wearing an unbelievable steampunk Peter Pan costume. Under the glittery makeup, his dark brown eyes and confident grin remind me of Devontae and I feel a tiny prick of guilt, remembering how our talk ended on Friday. I wonder how his rodeo went yesterday, and how we'll work on a class project together if we never speak to each other again. Why couldn't he have suggested going someplace a little more wheels-friendly?

Then Ale steps in a gopher hole as we're taking a shortcut to the back of the street of shops. "Ouch!" She grabs her ankle, hops around, then topples over.

There's no cell service down here, and Dad's nowhere in sight, so Ale sits on the ground, and Tina runs to the first aid tent. While we wait, Ale starts grilling me about Devontae.

"Why are you both acting like fools?" Ale's never been what you'd call subtle.

"Shouldn't you elevate your leg?" I dodge the question.

Ale wriggles over and props her leg in my lap.

"Seriously, though? First you spend half the week avoiding him. Then after school Friday, he looked like he couldn't get away from you fast enough. You're both being weird, chica."

Thankfully, Ale's lecture is cut short as Tina runs toward us, followed by a zombie fairy pulling a little red wagon. A sparkly sign that says YE OLDE FEY AMBULANCE is taped to the side.

"You've got to be kidding," Ale groans.

Turns out the bloodstained zombie fairy is a nurse. She pokes at Ale's ankle, then holds out her hands. "Up you go." She boosts Ale onto her good leg. "And in you go." She points at the wagon.

I try at least medium hard to keep from giggling as Ale is squeezed into ye olde ambulance, and Tina and I follow as the nurse trundles her to the medical tent.

Ale covers her eyes with her antennae. "I feel ridiculous!"

The nurse smirks, making her zombie makeup look even creepier. "Look around you!" she says, and waves a hand at the dressed-up, made-up, merry misfits that surround us.

She has a point. Nobody's paying us any mind. One thing I love about the festival is that pretty much nobody pays attention to my chair. It's almost like it's part of my costume—like those people riding in the wooden troll wagon or bouncing around on their spring-loaded stilts while telling fortunes. Everyone blends right in.

Ale sees the humor, and we all crack up. Her ankle's only twisted, and the nurse ices and wraps it for her, entertaining us with stories about all the weird injuries she's dealt with today.

"Next thing you know," she says as she finishes the neat wrap and tapes it in place, "the Mad Hatter trips, crashes into the Goblin King's stilt, and they both fly tush over teakettle!"

I laugh as hard as everyone, but I can't help comparing the reaction to Ale's fall to mine back at school. Why couldn't everyone just laugh that one off? It was a comedy of errors, too, thanks to good old Logan. We thank the nurse, who gives Ale crutches and tells her to ice again tonight and go easy a few days, then get back to window-shopping and creature watching.

We get to the music stage a little early, where a Celtic band is playing a set. The lead singer is dressed like a butterfly and spins as she sings, like she might take flight. People dance and twirl on the grass in front of the stage, caught up in the music. They make space for us, and we immediately start spinning and clapping with the crowd. Ale's bee antennae bobble as she hop-dances on her crutches. The song ends, and the one that follows makes me go cold.

It's a slower song that Mom used to play, and it floods me with memories. Past Fairy Festivals, how excited she'd get over the music and costumes.

Making music with her on our tiny back porch, her playing and me singing. The guitar Mom saved spare change in a coffee can a whole year to buy—little mother-of-pearl moons inlaid up the neck and the top printed with a picture of a lady in a boat she said was from a painting in some museum all the way over in Europe. She dreamed of going there one day to see it for real. *We'll need more than a coffee can to save all that change*, she'd joke, *but we'll do it*.

I was going to start lessons, too, before everything happened. Now the guitar hides in the closet, way back behind all those costumes.

As I blink hard, reminding myself it's only a song, I catch sight of Dad's green-and-brown tunic. He's standing behind the stage, near a little grove of trees hung with ribbons and charms to look like a fairy grotto. He's half turned toward the music, can't see me watching. The sunlight catches the tears sliding down his face before I can look away.

I freeze, the festival and the dancers spinning around me. Part of me wants to go over, to actually *talk* about Mom for once. To talk about *everything*. All the crap

I've been dealing with now, all the things we've never said before.

But that's not us.

I know how Dad deals. He gets things done, keeps things fixed. The more stressed he is, the faster he moves, always, *always*, pushing forward, never looking sideways or backward.

Also, if I watch him cry, I'll probably cry, too.

So I take a deep breath and get it together. Then I shove my wheels hard enough to set my chair spinning to the music again.

Like everything's just fine.

15

Shake It Off

Needless to say, Dad and I do not talk about what happened beside the stage when we get home. I take off my costume and makeup and undecorate my chair. We make dinner; then Dad heads across the yard to the shop with a textbook in his hand.

"Fun day, Emms," he says, dropping a kiss on my head as he leaves.

After he's gone, I try to focus on project brainstorming, organizing my supply boxes, and even cleaning the bathroom. I come up with zero project ideas, discover stink bugs in three of my Spanish moss packets, and vow to make Dad buy a shower curtain that's not a total disgrace.

Not even a brand-new WCMX video keeps my attention long—if anything, it makes my own wheelchair goal seem further away than ever. Am I kidding myself? Even if I do earn the money for that new chair, how much good is it going to do me if I can't so much as move between my classes at school without my Dawn shadow?

Also, how am I going to practice at all if Dad doesn't change his mind about the ramp in the field, and I have to keep sneaking around? All those cool videos I watch, and I've never seen one shot anyplace like where I live. It's all smooth concrete, curved wood, sleek cityscapes, and high-tech indoor arenas. Not one single ramp cobbled together from junk and plunked in a scrubby old field.

This isn't helping. I text Ale. **How's the ankle?**

Lots better. Doesn't even hurt much anymore, but Mom's been making my brothers wait on me since I got home, so they don't have to know that ☺. **I'm reading up on reverse hive splits while they burn dinner.**

Then:

You going to keep being weird around Devontae tomorrow?

We'll see, I reply. **Text SOS if I need to race over with the fire extinguisher.**

Then I log on and see my shop's been busy today. All three of the slightly snarky bags have sold, and a new review's gone up from AK_SalmonGranny. Five stars, but I'm a little disappointed she didn't leave a comment. I was half expecting something outrageous. I'm glad she liked her bag, though. I imagine her pulling some monster fish off a hook or sitting by a mountain or something, with my little bag tied onto her chair, flashing a metaphorical middle finger at anyone who stares at her wheels. Maybe one day I'll be that fearless.

I don't write customers after they've gotten their orders, unless there's a complaint, so I'm not sure why I send AK_SalmonGranny a short follow-up. Maybe leftover frustration that I never manage to talk to Dad about some of the bigger things. Maybe I don't want to think about the inevitable awkwardness with Devontae tomorrow, or another day with Dawn on my tail.

Whatever makes me do it, the message is nothing special. I thank her for the five-star review and ask if the bag was a good fit. She messages back almost immediately.

AK_SalmonGranny: LOVE the bag. Already got some memorable reactions ☺

HalfpipeEmms: ☺ I bet.

AK_SalmonGranny: The locals all know me. It's mostly the tourists that get all up in my business. Probably don't know any better, poor dears.

I know how that goes. It's a little different with people who know you.

HalfpipeEmms: You get weird looks for your wheels, too?

AK_SalmonGranny: Who doesn't?

HalfpipeEmms: ☺☺☺☺

I think about telling her how I almost didn't have the guts to make the bag at all, but then she writes more.

AK_SalmonGranny: I liked the new bags you put up—feisty!

HalfpipeEmms: You inspired me, I guess. They've already sold, too.

AK_SalmonGranny: Always happy to corrupt youth where I can. ☺

I'm surprised again at how much she doesn't sound like any grandparent—or other adult—I know. Except her sass reminds me a little of my mom, and maybe that's why I keep talking to her. One topic leads to another, and before I know it, I've told her all about the new chair I'm saving for, the Fairy Festival, and reluctantly helping Ale with her beehives while trying not to hyperventilate or crush stray bees with my wheels. And she tells me about her all-seniors, nonmotorized touring group (Purgatory's Pixies), seven ways to cook salmon, and how she first came to Alaska as a can-can dancer way back when she was just eighteen.

She's so much fun to talk to, I'm surprised when I hear Dad come inside almost an hour later. I'm even more surprised to realize I feel a whole lot better—even though it's so late I once again don't get a chance to tell Dad about Dawn.

The next morning, I arrive at school determined to try and be a bit more like AK_SalmonGranny and not let anyone or anything get to me.

I also vow to suck it up and straighten things out with Devontae.

It takes almost all day to get some time without Dawn over my shoulder. Finally, after I'm done eating and she goes on lunch break, I break away and find Devontae in the library again, reading a rodeo magazine. He doesn't look up, even though I know he hears my wheels rasp over the carpet.

I stop in front of him. "Got a minute?"

"Just about." Devontae looks up from the book but doesn't smile. "What's up?"

My fingers fidget with my brakes, flipping them on and off and on again. "The rodeo. How'd you do?"

He gives me a funny look. "You interested for real?"

"Yeah. I wanted to come, too."

"Could've fooled me." Now Devontae closes his book and starts to stand up.

I make myself keep talking. "I did. I just couldn't."

Devontae looks confused.

"Okay, okay. The truth? I don't go to Setzler's Arena. Ever."

Devontae slowly sits back down. "Because you hate rodeo?"

Just say it. "Because of the bathrooms."

"The bathrooms?" he repeats. Glory, I'm going to have to spell it out.

"Porta-potties aren't the most *accessible* spots on the planet." I point to my wheels with both hands, in case he's 100 percent dense, then make for the door before I discover if you can literally die of embarrassment.

Halfway there, Devontae catches me. "I'm a jerk, okay?" He takes a knee so we're eye to eye. "I didn't think about that."

"Most people don't."

"I won," Devontae says suddenly.

"Huh?"

"You asked how I did. I won." Devontae's not one to big himself up, but the pride on his face is clear. Makes me wish I'd been there to see him ride.

"You get another big, shiny buckle?" I work hard to sound only low-key interested.

He shrugs, working hard to look modest. "Medium shiny. So, we good?"

"We're good." Telling him wasn't quite as awful as I'd feared, and I feel better now.

"Great. Now can we stop stalling on this project, or what?" he says. "Not that I'm dying to do homework, but I only get to ride as long as my grades stay up."

Then, of course, Dawn runs into the library and scurries over like she's found the missing crown jewels. Before she can embarrass me too badly, I tell her we're talking homework, and she at least goes and sits at another table.

When she's out of earshot, Devontae leans over. "What's with the new supervisor?"

I roll my eyes and whisper back the highlights. Devontae winces like a horse just stomped his newest pair of boots.

"Dang," he says. "No way out of it?"

"Trust me, I'm working on it."

Devontae makes a scrunched-up thinking face. "Why don't we work at my house? She can't follow you there, right?" he adds, his eyes going wide at the thought.

I laugh. "No! I leave her at the door at three thirty." The idea of working on our project at his house is both nerve-racking and exciting. We agree to work it out with our parents and meet next week.

"Okay, then." Devontae hops to his purple-and-green-booted feet, and we head out of the library, Dawn trailing a few paces behind. Halfway down the hall,

Devontae leans over and whispers, "I feel like I'm in some spy movie."

"Tell me about it." I fill him in on the mild mayhem I've been committing all week to help Dawn earn her paycheck, and he gets a look on his face that my mom would have called puckish.

"You know . . ." he says slowly, and I can almost see an idea blooming in his brain. "Maybe you could switch up your approach."

"How do you mean?"

He waves the magazine he's still holding. There's a cowboy on the front, holding tight as a tick to a bucking horse.

"When I climb onto a bronc, I don't want any one-trick pony. No challenge—no fun. The best ones always keep you guessing. Which way will they buck? Will they twist-and-shimmy or use the same old moves?"

"What am I, a horse?"

"Not exactly." He laughs. "But you know what horses do when they don't want that rider on their back, right?"

"*Ah.*" The light bulb goes on.

"Shake it *off.*"

16

Evasive Action

Two days later, Operation See Dawn Run is officially launched.

Ale and Devontae meet me outside school as soon as my dad pulls away. Instead of following the crowd through the front door, where Dawn waits for me beside the office, we cut through the parking lot to the doors by the cafeteria that stay locked in the morning. Ale knocks twice, and Tina pushes the door open from inside. Markus and Zeke are with her.

"At your service, Lady Emmie," Zeke jokes as I pop over the threshold into the deserted hallway. "For all your mischief and mayhem needs."

Devontae catches my eye and winks. "Ready for action?"

My friends form a loose huddle with me hidden at the center, and we weave into the crowded main hallway. Our plan works—Dawn has no idea I've ditched her, and my crew drops Tina and me off at homeroom, promising to be back at the bell. I hustle to my desk, avoiding Tina's eyes so we don't start laughing.

Dawn slips in two minutes after the bell, looking confused.

"Did I miss you?" she whispers as she brings a chair over and sits.

I shrug, eyes wide. "Got here same time as usual—didn't see you."

Three seats away, Tina has a sudden coughing fit.

Five minutes before the end of class, I casually pack up my things.

I also slide Dawn's phone from her open purse onto the floor.

When the bell screams, I bolt for the door while Dawn's still gathering her purse and jacket. Tina stays right behind me, and she's somehow spread the word, because a clear path to the door magically opens for me. Our friends are waiting. They close around me again, and we race away. I'm settled at my second-period desk by the time Dawn comes puffing in. This time she looks a little annoyed but still doesn't say anything. Near the end of class, she realizes her phone's gone, so she panics and goes to check homeroom. The bell rings again, and I'm out of there before she reappears.

We keep it up all day. At lunch, the six of us can barely keep a straight face. Dawn, who's managed to find her phone, is typing furiously on it in the corner of the cafeteria. I can tell she still isn't exactly sure if this is all coincidence or on purpose, but she's not quite her usual syrup-sweet self.

We do it again the next day. After dismissal, Mr. Milling asks me to hold up a second before I leave his class.

"Go ahead, Ms. Wanamaker," he tells Dawn. "I have to stop at the office, so Emmie and I can head that way together."

"Bye, Emmie!" Dawn chirps, like we haven't led her on another day-long scavenger hunt. Maybe she's afraid of Dr. Grayling learning she's no good at her job if she tells on me.

When she's gone, Mr. Milling perches on the desk beside mine, spinning a pencil through his fingers. "How're things going, Emmie?"

"Fine," I answer quickly. "I like your class."

"Glad to hear it." Mr. Milling sticks the pencil into his thick, dreadlocked ponytail. "You like history, don't you?"

"I do." I'm not a huge reader, but Mr. Milling makes everything we learn super interesting.

"Speaking of history, that's an impressive testudo you and your team pulled off."

"Testudo?"

Mr. Milling whips the pencil from his hair, scribbles the word onto a sticky note, and hands it to me. I wonder if he's about to call me out on shaking Dawn. But he hops up, straightens some things on his desk, and heads to the door of the portable, nodding at me to follow.

He doesn't butt in as I go down the ramp—even when I have to slow down for a warped floorboard—and makes small talk as we cross the courtyard. But when we reach the front doors, he asks how Devontae and me are doing on our project.

"Getting it together," I assure him. "Got a study session planned."

"I'm not worried," he replies.

My dad's truck is waiting outside, and Mr. Milling pushes the door open for me in a smooth, polite way—like he'd do for ladies at church or a granddad juggling groceries. As I roll out, I turn back to tell him thanks, but he's already headed up the hall.

Without stopping at the office.

Dad's home three evenings in a row. He catches up on some projects around the house, and we hang out and catch up on each other. He does some minor maintenance on my wheels, and we have a bad-movie marathon with popcorn and hot chocolate. Every sensible part of my brain tells me this is the time to start the conversation about Dawn. But every time I start to, I chicken out. Having Dad around—so much like old times—feels too good to wreck.

We spend Thursday afternoon fishing down at Nelson's pond.

"Been too long since we did this." Dad slides a night crawler onto his hook and makes a perfect cast into the still, dark water.

"Yep." I gulp a handful of chips and reel in my line to discover something's swiped my bait. The gentle breeze and soft, late-day sun filtering through the branches above us make me feel too relaxed to focus on fishing, but I don't even care. It's been so nice to hang out together like this. All the stress of school and Dawn and Dr. Grayling and wondering if Dad's pushing himself too hard at work melts away as we sit under the big, drooping live oak and listen to crickets chirping and our lines plunking in the water.

"How's it going with the aide?" Dad asks suddenly. The happy and relaxed look on his face starts slipping away.

I want to tell him about it so bad. How frustrated

I feel when she grabs my chair and pushes me over thresholds I can manage myself. How kids have already started treating me different—like I'm not the same Emmie they've known forever. Like we can't talk about much of anything because Dawn's always right there, hearing everything.

But Dad hasn't looked relaxed for so long, and I remember how out of place and twitchy he was at that last meeting. Things seem to be settling down, a bit. Maybe I can last a while longer—at least until I know Dad's class is going better. Besides, Operation See Dawn Run is already running her ragged—maybe she'll up and quit on her own if we keep it up. So I fib.

"She's not my favorite, but it's no big deal," I tell him. My line *whirrrr*s through the air as I make another cast.

Dad doesn't look convinced. "We can still talk to the school," he says. His line jerks, and he starts working it in. Then I get a bite, and we both have to hustle so the fish don't tangle our lines.

When we've each landed a nice-size bass for the cooler and rebaited our hooks, Dad seems to have forgotten about Dawn, and I still can't bring myself to ruin the best day—and week—we've had in a long, long time by reminding him. Especially since tomorrow will be here way too soon.

"You know what tomorrow is, right?"

My head snaps up, and I fumble my cast. The line spins off the reel way too fast, like it wants to avoid Dad's words as much as I do.

I make myself reel it in slowly and try again. "I know."

When Dad doesn't say more, I make myself look over. He's staring intently at the pond, watching a pair of green-winged teals poking around in the reeds on the far shore.

Tomorrow is Mom's birthday. The first year she was gone, Dad and I were too hunkered down in survival mode to do much more than make it through the day. Last year, Nonny took over, insisting it was only proper that we do something. *To show respect.*

"Is Nonny making us go to the cemetery?" I finally ask.

Dad slowly reels in his line and sighs. "You got it."

The next day, Dad leaves work early, collects me from school, and we meet Nonny and Pop-Pop at Holy Cross Cemetery.

Maybe it's weird, but I actually like Holy Cross. I mean, if you have to spend eternity dirt-napping in some cemetery, this one isn't so bad. It's tucked away on a backroad, with big, shady trees over the tombstones and concrete angels and flower wreaths. I've seen some cemeteries stuck right beside the interstate, which Mom would have hated.

Nonny's already pulling potted flowers and tools from her trunk and piling them up in Pop-Pop's arms.

"I got enough for all of us," Nonny says as we get out and join them. "Fortunately."

Dad's face tightens. "Looks nice." He doesn't say much else as we gather up the flowers and tools and bring them to Mom's grave.

I haven't been here in a while, but I can tell Nonny has, because the gladioluses planted there are freshly weeded and watered. She doesn't waste time—spreads a cloth, plunks down a foam pad for her knees, and starts digging holes for the fresh plants and bulbs we've brought like it's a mission. Dad has his clippers, and he trims a few overhanging branches from the nearby trees. Pop-Pop starts to sneeze from all the fresh-cut grass, so he walks a few rows over to visit some of his friends who already live here.

I watch Dad and Nonny work for a bit; then the long, smooth pathways that cut through the gravestones start tempting me. Mom wouldn't have minded me taking advantage of them, so I cut loose a bit.

When I pop a wheelie—just a little one—Nonny fusses at me to stop.

"Have some respect, Emelyn—we're here to visit your mother, not cut up."

I bite my lip to stop from pointing out that Mom would have liked seeing how good I've gotten at that long-distance wheelie.

"Leave her be, Lula," Dad says briskly. "She's not hurting anything. Let her deal with things her way."

Nonny stabs her trowel into the sandy ground. "She needs to learn respect."

"She's not your daughter, Lula." Dad's voice is cold and tight. My head whips around—so does Pop-Pop's—to see them facing off in front of Mom's headstone, almost stepping on the new flowers.

"No, Alan. She's yours. You're her father, not her friend. Sometimes I think you forget."

"Lula . . ." Dad's voice is like a too-tight bungee cord, about to snap.

Nonny doubles down. "Why didn't you tell me Emelyn had a fall at school? Why did I have to hear about that from Etta Wanamaker at church?"

"What business is it of Etta Wanamaker's?" Dad's head might fly off, he looks so mad.

"Her daughter is Emelyn's new aide." Nonny shoots her words like an archery champ. "Emelyn's apparently been making things miserable for her. With poor

Etta's health what it's been lately, it's driving Dawn to distraction!"

Distracted from what? I almost ask, but then Nonny's words make me think about how Dawn's always so superglued to her phone. I wonder for a guilty second if it's because her mom's having more medical problems.

Trust Nonny to pick up gossip and then keep it back for ammunition. I don't know why Etta Wanamaker shared my business at church, or if Dawn's actually "driven to distraction" by a couple harmless pranks.

Either way, isn't this day hard enough already?

I spin a 180 and take off down the path between the gravestones so fast my shoulders burn. It's twisty, though, and Pop-Pop catches up by cutting through the grass.

"Hold up, Biscuit," he says quietly. "Let's you and me take a detour. Let them have it out."

Pop-Pop's voice is calm, reassuring. I slow down enough so he can keep up, and we move farther into the cemetery, past a cluster of pink- and red-blooming crape myrtle trees. I try to block out the angry voices behind us as Dad and Nonny go at it.

"This isn't about you, Biscuit." Pop-Pop hums a little song like we're out for any old stroll. "Just so you know."

I know there's a lot going on here. Nonny disapproving that Dad and I didn't bring flowers to put on Mom's grave. Dad wanting so bad to tell Nonny to mind her own business about how we choose to grieve. They used to get along okay when Mom was still alive, but that's all long gone. Dad hates being told what to do so much he'd rather cut off his own foot than wear a shoe someone else picked for him. Like me, I guess.

Sometimes I think, under all those critical frowns and forced family dinners, Nonny's bone-deep scared we're going to forget Mom if she doesn't keep reminding us.

"I hate when they fight," I finally say.

"Me too." Pop-Pop sighs. "Grief can hurt twice, Biscuit. Hurts the one feeling it, always. Then sometimes folks board it up instead of looking it in the face—then it hurts everyone the second time around when it comes crashing out. Even people we love most. *Especially* them."

I don't say anything, but the smooth pavement under my wheels is soothing, and Pop-Pop's words make a weird kind of sense. I guess I'm not the only one in this family who goes for evasive action sometimes.

Not sure it's working so well for any of us these days.

17

Sewing (and Preconceived) Notions

I spend Saturday morning filling orders and making more bags. The sassy ones have turned into my top sellers, so the embroidery function on my sewing machine—and my shaky lettering skills—gets a good workout as I whip up a half dozen more.

By lunchtime, I've accidentally stitched my fingers twice, but the red in my wall thermometer has climbed another forty-six dollars. I've also run out of red, blue, and purple thread, so I get Dad to drive me the six miles from our place to the Dollar General.

"I'll grab you in half an hour, Emms," he calls as he pulls away. We haven't mentioned his dustup with Nonny yesterday.

We live way out, so *shopping* is a relative term—on one side of the county road is the hair salon and an exterminator. The other side has the Dollar General and the hardware store. Because Dad's a creature of habit, I know he'll go get his hair cut, grab an iced tea at the gas station, and hang out at the hardware store for fifteen minutes before he collects me.

I wave goodbye and roll toward the Dollar General, which sits in what used to be a cow pasture and looks a little strange with other fields—and cows—still all bunched up close around it. Strange or not, it's nice not to have to drive twenty miles to get some groceries anymore, and I can get a lot of the basic stuff I need for my bags right here. They have an okay selection of fabrics, ribbons, and some sewing supplies. There's also the big, smooth parking lot with low, concrete parking dividers—of course, I can't resist a few pops and hops.

Nobody fusses at me to be careful. Nobody rushes over to grab my chair—even when I do a long, scraping ride balanced along the length of the longest low divider. It's glorious.

Then I race inside, through the one wonderful automatic door in a fifteen-mile radius, past scarecrows and pumpkins and Halloween costumes. I pick out my thread and add some spools of ribbon with spiderwebs and ghosts and a few Halloween fabric remnants.

Maybe I'll add some holiday bags to the shop, since we're heading into that season.

I get back to the lot with ten minutes to spare before Dad picks me up, so I stow my loot in my chair bag and roll around to the field-facing side of the building where almost nobody parks. I work some more hops and pops over the curb, then get a little fancier. The space from the curb to the first low divider isn't that wide. I go halfway down the narrow sidewalk that runs along the building, turn, and wheel as hard as I can to gather speed.

I nail it. Just enough air to bridge the gap and clear the divider with only the tiniest impact of my back tires against the concrete. I pop a victory wheelie and hop a few times, my heart pounding and feeling better than I have in a long time.

"That was amazing!"

I know that voice. I let my wheels bang down and whip around. Dawn's standing there, holding a loaded shopping bag and looking impressed.

I'm torn between feeling a little irritated that she's been watching me . . . and proud that someone saw me land that little jump. Especially someone whose whole job is basically keeping me from doing things myself.

Pride wins. "Thanks," I tell her.

I remember what Nonny said in the cemetery yesterday about Dawn's momma not doing so good health-wise. I wonder again, with a guilty little stab, if that's why Dawn's always watching her phone like a buzzard over roadkill.

There's an awkward silence. Finally, Dawn asks, "You here by yourself?"

"My dad'll be right back. I stopped in to grab some supplies."

"Party supplies?"

"Sewing supplies." I pull out the roll of spider-printed ribbon and show it to her.

"Ooh." Dawn runs a fingernail over the sparkles. "I love notions." She must see from my face that I don't know what she means, so she explains that *notions* are sewing things like ribbons and thread. The only notions I knew about were the kind Mom used to call preconceived notions, which is when you make a snap judgment about something or someone before getting the full story. Like how people who first meet me assume I can't do things for myself, or order my own food.

Or, I guess, how I've sort of assumed Dawn isn't worth getting to know. As much fun as I've had giving her the slip this week, I know deep down Mom probably wouldn't be proud of me for that—especially since we might be skimming a fine line between funny and mean.

"Emmie," Dawn asks suddenly, "did I do something that upset you?"

Her directness catches me off guard. "What do you mean?" I hedge.

"You haven't exactly tried to hide it," she points out.

My face gets hot as I realize maybe Dawn hasn't been quite as clueless as we figured. She looks more interested than angry, though.

"Why haven't you told on me?" I ask, actually curious now.

Dawn shrugs. "I'm a big girl," she says. "Also, to be honest—I need this job. Having to play a bit of chase isn't going to change that."

"Because of your mom?" I ask without thinking.

Dawn looks surprised, but nods. "Yeah. Hate leaving her home alone all day, but medical bills have piled up lately. That's why I was so grateful when this job came up."

Now I feel flat-out guilty about the stunts we've pulled. Especially since Dawn seems to be talking to me for real right now.

I decide to try being nice, too. "Do you sew, too?" I ask, since she was so interested in the ribbons and fabric I bought. Also, a little bit, to change the subject.

She doesn't, but she uses ribbons and buttons and fancy paper in the scrapbooks she makes, which I didn't know was even a thing. Then she asks more about the stunts I was doing with my chair.

"I didn't know you could do things like that with a wheelchair," she says.

"Got your phone?" I ask, and when she hands it to me, I show her a couple WCMX videos. When they're done, she looks at me almost like she's seeing me for the first time.

"Is it dangerous?" she asks.

"Not if you know what you're doing." I shrug. "Like any sport."

Dawn's quiet a second. Then she asks if I'm using the sewing supplies I bought for more chair bags, and before I even realize what I'm doing, I tell her about how I'm saving for a new chair, one that's better equipped for jumps and tricks. When I show her the online specs—and the price tag—her eyes widen.

"That's such a lot of money," she says. "How long will it take you?"

I start to tell her that my shop's doing well and that I've already saved up nearly half of what I need, but then Dad's truck pulls into the lot. So I tell her goodbye and head over to meet him, holding my bag of sewing notions and wondering if maybe my preconceived ones were a tiny bit wrong.

18

Shuri Says . . .

Devontae's house sure is nice. It's one of the new brick places that went up along County Route 6 a few years back. His is neat and square and surrounded by small paddocks that line the long driveway. Four young pecan trees dot the yard in front of the house.

Devontae directs my dad around to a sliding-glass door that doesn't have any steps. Dad tells me to study hard, waves at Devontae, and leaves.

Everything inside is new and shiny—matching living room furniture, gleaming kitchen, and little light-rainbows glittering from the glass fixture over the dinner table. No wonder Devontae can buy so many fancy boots. The floors are smooth tile. Even better, the first-floor bathroom has a big, open design.

"Come on," Devontae says when he's finished showing me around. "Let's eat!"

Dinner's fantastic—Beaufort stew that's heavy on the shrimp, light on the potatoes, and perfectly spicy—but

I spend the whole meal stressing that I might accidentally chip one of the thin, delicate plates. Devontae's family is so much fun. He has three much-older sisters, two in college nearby and one who's a nurse up in Charlotte but comes home weekends. His mom works at the bank, and his dad teaches at the same college his sisters go to. Dinner's way louder and livelier than at my place. Mrs. Washington watches my plate like a hawk, and soon I'm begging her to stop reloading.

"If I don't quit, I'll end up with two flat tires," I finally protest, when all else fails.

There's a pause, as everyone wonders if it's okay to laugh at a wheelchair joke, even if I'm the one who made it. Then Mr. Washington grins.

"I like this girl, Tae," he declares.

Before long, I'm feeling right at home with these chatty, friendly people, and it makes me think about how quiet things have been at home lately.

Devontae's grandma, Momma Rose, hasn't said much during dinner. Then, as we're all scraping pecan pie from our dessert plates, she turns to me.

"Your momma was a Wolfe, wasn't she?"

"Jeannie Wolfe, ma'am," I answer. "Before she got married."

Devontae throws his mom a look. "Momma Rose . . ." he says, real low.

She ignores him. "I remember you, child," she tells me. "I was secretary at the clinic where your momma used to bring you for therapy when you were a tiny thing." Then she squints at Devontae.

"You never said you were bringing a girl home."

Everything goes sort of quiet. I stare at the rips in my jeans, wondering what that means. Is she surprised that he's brought a girl home? Or that the girl he brought is *me*?

Devontae looks ready to dive under the table. "We're *studying*."

Mr. Washington cuts in. "Momma, have more pie."

"Mmm-*hmm*." Momma Rose takes the pie and doesn't say much more, but I feel her gaze roaming down to my chair and back up to my face while we finish up dessert. Tasty as it is, I have to swallow a couple extra times to get the last of my pie down under the weight of her eyes.

The second we finish, Devontae all but knocks his chair over leaping up. "Study time!" he announces, a little too loud. "Want to meet my horse first?"

His parents excuse us, and his sisters shoot us sympathetic looks as we make for the door.

Out in the super-clean stable, rows of ribbons and certificates line one wall. Devontae's been stacking up the first-place wins. We're both too embarrassed to say much for a few moments, but Devontae finally goes first.

"Sorry about that," he says, shaking his head and running a hand over his hair. "Momma Rose sort of says whatever comes to mind."

"That's okay," I tell him. "My nonny's about the same." Which is pretty much true, though Nonny mostly disapproves of Dad and me on general principles, while I'm not sure what Momma Rose was thinking when she looked at me.

I finally convince Devontae it's no big deal, and he introduces me to Shuri, his horse, which smooths things out. I haven't spent much time quite this close to a horse, and having her smooth gray-dappled side right at my eye line is a little intimidating, even with the fence rails between us. But then Shuri sticks her nose in my lap and slobbers my shirt, which Devontae says means we're friends.

"Okay," I finally say, getting back to why we're here. "Project time?" We're both solid B students, and I know for a fact he'd pick being out on some horse over doing homework any day—just like I'd sooner be popping ramps.

"Guess so." Devontae pulls out some comb things and shows me how to brush Shuri's shiny coat through the fence rails while we brainstorm. It's slow and rhythmic and gives my hands something to do besides fidgeting on my wheels. The project isn't hard, exactly, but it's going to be a lot of work. We have to choose six real people who were—or are—in Mr. Milling's word, groundbreakers. Then we have to make a whole presentation where we imagine them all having a conversation together—one that brings in important things about what makes each one of them groundbreaking and what challenges they had to face down along the way. As usual for Mr. Milling's assignments, grades include "extra points for passion."

"Trust Mr. Milling to bend our brains," Devontae says, as we both toss out random ideas and he saves them in his phone. We get as far as Bill Pickett (Devontae), Danica Patrick (me), and Dr. Ron McNair (obvious, since he was hands down the most famous person from around here).

Then the conversation sort of naturally slides over to school news and gossip. Then we stop talking altogether, and the only sound is the *shh-shh* of the brushes through Shuri's soft hair. It's comfortable silence, but I can't help wondering if I'm the only one feeling this tiny flutter whenever we're around each other.

We finish combing Shuri's coat and feed her some treats. Then we watch as she wanders back out to the paddock, swishing her long tail.

Ale has her older sisters and her aunties to ask about all this boy nonsense—and her mom. I wish I could ask my mom, too, because it sure is tough trying to figure it all out on my own.

To clear my head, I pop a few hops over the concrete stable floor. That turns into a full-on spin. I don't stop whirling, around and around, until I'm dizzy.

When I finally stop, Devontae whistles. "I love how you work those wheels, Emmie," he says. "You look like how I feel when I climb onto a bronc."

He called me Emmie. Not Hot Wheels. Not Em.

By the time Dad comes to collect me, we've come up with four people to use for our project, and we agree to each figure out one more to add by the end of next week, which is when our final list is due. Good thing we have a couple months to work on this, because we've got to be in the running for slowest team ever.

"Have fun?" Dad asks as we drive home through the early fall twilight.

Parts of it were a little stressful—like Momma Rose looking me over with eagle eyes and feeling a bit out of place in their fancy house. But the rest—meeting Shuri, talking about famous people we admire, getting to meet Devontae's family and see what he's like when he isn't at the laughing center of his group of friends— all of that was jam up.

"Yeah. It was good."

Later that night, a message chimes on my tablet as I'm getting ready for bed.

Broncs&Boots: Shuri says you should come over again sometime. If you want.

Well, after that, it's past midnight before I can fall asleep.

19

Tortoise to Jackrabbit

What with dinner at Devontae's and trying to figure out what that message from "Shuri" was all about, it takes me until Sunday afternoon to remember to look up what Mr. Milling meant when he said my friends and me had pulled off an impressive whatever he called it. I dig through the dirty clothes basket to find the pants pocket with the paper he scribbled the word on—luckily, nobody's done the wash yet.

testudo (n) | te-'stü-(,)dō
pl: testudos
Def: A cover of overlapping shields or a shed
wheeled up to a wall used by the ancient
Romans to protect against an attacking force.
Latin: *testudin-, testudo*, tortoise, tortoise
shell.

I have to laugh once I see what the word means—a packed-together group of soldiers, moving along in sync with their shields out and overlapped, making an enemy-proof place to hide inside or fight from. He could have just said he saw how they all clumped up to hide me from Dawn, but I guess that's what makes him one of my favorite teachers. I get his point, but the testudo we've made is a whole lot faster than any old tortoise.

I *know* it's a little unfair—how we've kept Dawn hopping from the first bell to the last, especially after our conversation at the Dollar General yesterday. She's cooler than I thought—a little—and I know it's not her fault I got stuck with an aide. I do. But right now, it's about the only thing I feel like I have any control over at school.

Besides, she didn't seem too fussed about it.

So we keep it up on Monday . . . but not quite as much as before. A few escapes here and there, enough to give me some breathing room—not quite enough that I can't play it off as an accident.

We do the same thing on Tuesday. And on Wednesday.

Then on Wednesday evening, just as I'm getting ready to finally settle in and work a little on Mr. Milling's project, a letter from school turns up in the mail.

Dad's home early, and he finds the envelope in the

stack of junk mail before I can intercept it. I watch him rip it open, wondering nervously if Ms. Hernandez wrote it, if I'm about to get into trouble over what we've been doing after all.

Dad reads the letter, and his eyebrows about climb off his face, which makes me fear the worst. Then I realize Dad looks thoughtful, not mad. Did Ms. Hernandez write to tell Dad I don't need an aide after all?

"Hey, Emms," he says slowly, setting down the letter. "Looks like that new chair of yours might turn up sooner than later."

The bad news: I still have an aide.

The good news: I'm not in trouble.

The *weird* news: The school wants to hold a fundraiser for my new wheels.

It was all spelled out in that letter from Dr. Grayling— or his secretary. Dad and I need to let them know exactly which chair and specs we want and give them pictures and prices. Wheelchairs this specialized have tons of custom parts, so this is important—I should maybe even get on the phone with someone from the company, make sure I choose the right specs.

Then they're going to raise the money.

And then I'll hit send on the order for my dream set

of wheels. And I'll finally be able to show everyone what I can do. Myself included.

Dad reads the letter out loud. Then he frowns, sort of smiles, and carefully folds and unfolds the letter like it might explode. Finally, he sets it aside and looks at me.

"What do you think, Emms?"

I'm already bubbling with excitement. All those months and months of stuffing tangly Spanish moss into little bags, chopping and bundling sticky slivers of pine wood, and stitching letters and trims and patches onto chair bags—sometimes it felt like *I* was the tortoise, inching along toward some distant, sparkly finish line I couldn't even quite see. Now I'm about to morph into a jackrabbit.

All at once, I can almost feel a rush of wind and sun in my face, hear the thrum of wood and concrete under those monster oversize, knobby tires, and feel those chunky handrims spinning through my fingers as I make a perfect launch into midair . . .

Even better, getting that chair should definitely be enough to get me out from under a babysitter at school. Even Dr. Grayling will have to realize that once he sees the chair I've picked out and everything I'll be able to do with it. Liability stickler or not, nobody can help being convinced by gear this good. I might not have to get Dad involved at all, which would honestly probably be easier.

I grab the letter off the coffee table and scan it myself to be sure it's the real deal.

"I think . . . maybe it's about time to start choosing those specs."

I'm so excited by this surprise news that it isn't until morning that it occurs to me to wonder why the school decided to raise money for my chair—or how they even knew about the chair at all. I spend some time chasing down the details, and by the end of the day, I think I've got it straight. As far as I can piece together, here's what happened.

After Dawn saw me doing tricks off the curbs and over the parking barriers in the Dollar General lot, she happened to mention it in the employee break room at school, where Mr. Singletary heard her and chimed in that I've been doing tricks with him during open gym. Ms. Hernandez was there, too, and very interested to know what I've been up to outside school.

She must have talked to Dr. Grayling. Because somehow, somebody had the idea to start a schoolwide fundraiser for my new ride.

I'm not sure why Dawn would want to help me get a new chair when I haven't made her job very easy—even if I have been a little nicer the past few days. Or Dr. Grayling.

Mr. Singletary and Ms. Hernandez make more sense, though, and Ms. Parsons is probably all for it. Come to think of it, maybe she even told them about my broken armrest being partly to blame for my tumble on the ramp—even though it's fixed now.

It's all still a tiny bit weird. But I'm so excited that I don't give it much more than a passing thought.

Guess it's so long, tortoise . . . hello, jackrabbit.

20

A Lucky Thing

For a few days after that letter arrives, I'm too excited to focus on much of anything else. I manage to stay half-way on top of my homework and keep things picked up around the house enough to prevent total chaos. I let the online shop go almost completely, other than wrapping up a few pending orders and mailing them off. I don't post anything new for sale.

I guess I don't need to anymore.

I can't disappear into Stunt Chair Dreamland for-ever, though. So, after giving myself a few days to geek out over components and colors and about a million little added extras, I agree to help Ale study for her first-level beekeeping exam, which is next week. Just the information on the written test, thank goodness. No risking life and limb like last time.

"Nurse, house, guard . . ." Ale drums her heels against the wall and looks at me upside down. She's draped over my bed and ticking off different types of worker bees on her fingers. "Scout and . . . forager!" she finishes triumphantly.

I double-check the brick-size book she's studying from. "You got it. I don't think you need to worry about this."

"You can never be too prepared," Ale insists. "Everyone else taking this test is, like, older than thirty. I have to prove myself."

Ale never quite believes she's as smart as she is. So, even though it's super boring, I quiz her for another twenty minutes or so. When she's finally satisfied she's made enough progress, we go out to the kitchen to scrounge some snacks.

"What frame did you pick?" Ale studies the printouts I've left scattered over the table.

"Still choosing." I balance a bag of chips and a bowl on my lap and dig in the fridge for some salsa. "Either Electric Grape or Poison Apple." I point to my favorite color samples—one's deep, sparkling purple shot with cloudy silver streaks; the other's a twist of neon green and candy red. Arctic Blast—pearl white swirled with glittery black—is in third place.

"So many cool options." Ale devours a handful of chips. "It's like choosing a bike or a dress, isn't it?"

"Only way cooler." I show her a couple more printouts with different tire choices and the option to have my name threaded into the back of the seat in any color. I might be getting a little too old for that, though. I don't bother mentioning the even bigger decisions about cambers and casters and roll bars—even if I did just spend half an hour reading questions about bugs.

"This still feels wild." Ale shuffles the pictures. "You're actually going to get this! Like, soon! I guess you won't need to keep up with the shop anymore," she adds, looking bummed.

I suddenly remember she's only halfway to earning her custom beehive house and then feel bad that I sort of forgot.

"Maybe not as much," I tell her. "But I still want to." I might hold off on the bags for now. They take time to make—time I could be using to practice tricks. Maybe I could keep collecting and selling the other things, though, to help Ale.

After we finish our snack, we head back to my room and start posting more pine cones and moss packs in the online shop.

"So. Dinner at Rodeo Prince's place." Ale gives me her detective look. "Tell."

"Not much to tell." I hope my face isn't as red as the Poison Apple wheelchair frame. "Food was great. Worked on our project. Brushed his horse."

"That's it?" Ale's clearly unconvinced.

"There was pecan pie—even better than Nonny's."

Ale rolls her eyes. "Well? You like him or what?"

"I guess, sure. Everyone likes him, right?"

"Yes. That's exactly what I meant, Emmie." Ale tosses some Spanish moss at me. "That's totally why I've seen you two playing ball in the gym three mornings in a row when I get to school."

"Half the kids who come early play ball in the gym," I point out, even though that's not completely true.

"Not one-on-one."

I can *feel* my face flush Poison Apple red. Ale: 1. Emmie: 0.

I'm not being cagey. I don't *know* what I think about Devontae. Sure, he's cute and nice, but everyone knows that. It was fun hanging out and brushing Shuri while we talked about our project. The blushes I have to hide whenever he smiles at me sure haven't gone anywhere.

Once again, I wish I could talk to someone who actually understands things like this. How do you know if you like someone? How do you know if they like you back?

And if you do, and they do . . . what the heck are you supposed to do then?

I can't tell Ale that, because she'd run and get one of her older sisters or her younger aunties, and it'd turn into some whole big thing.

Instead, I grab her bee book and start asking the hardest questions I can find. After ten in a row she gets one wrong and starts to panic that she's not ready for her test. She starts rereading a chapter she already knows cold, and I gather up the new supplies we've collected and log on to update our listings. There's another message in my inbox.

AK_SalmonGranny: Haven't seen any new bags in your shop lately. Was planning to buy one for a buddy of mine, will there be more?

HalfpipeEmms: Actually, that might be on hold for a bit.

A pause.

AK_SalmonGranny: Not working toward the new chair anymore?

HalfpipeEmms: No. Yes. Well, sort of.

Since this seems like the sort of thing she'd like, I type a quick message filling her in on the letter from the school and the planned fundraiser to get me my new wheels. I hit send, expecting some sort of sassy answer.

The computer goes silent for a few minutes. Then her reply chimes in.

AK_SalmonGranny: Well. Isn't that a lucky thing?

Then, before I can write anything back, another message follows the last one.

AK_SalmonGranny: Did I miss something, or weren't you doing fine earning that chair on your own?

21

Those Crafty Fighters

All through the next day, AK_SalmonGranny's message stays lodged in a corner of my mind like a treble hook snagged in a bass's fin. I thought she'd be happy to hear I was getting my new chair way ahead of schedule, but she sounded almost disappointed.

The fundraiser makes the morning loudspeaker announcements, and by noon, plenty of kids and teachers have come up to me in class or the halls to talk about it. It's kind of nice how excited everyone sounds.

I make a special effort to be nice to Dawn. Now that it won't be long until everyone sees I don't need her, it can't hurt to get along in the meantime. Also, I guess she's sort of the reason this is even happening. So I try to think of things to talk about while we're in the halls between classes, and I don't hide her phone. Even when she leaves it right on top of the desk and it would be so, so easy.

When Ale and Tina ask when we're planning our next disappearing act, I tell them to hold off for now.

"No more testudo?" Tina looks disappointed.

"Not right now," I tell her, then try not to cringe when Logan Whitten walks up and starts talking to her. I have no idea how, but Tina and Logan seem to be striking up a friendship. I'm trying not to feel annoyed by that; I know Tina can be friends with whoever she wants. I just wish it could've been *anyone* but Logan.

I don't show how I truly feel, though. Even when Logan makes a point of bringing up how much it hurt when I whacked his knees on the ramp that day.

I do not point out that he was the one who got all up in my space in the first place.

I do not knock him down and then leave tire marks up and down his scrawny self.

I am calm. Mature.

When nobody else is looking, Devontae makes a funny face at me behind Logan's back, and my angry thoughts all sort of melt away. Halfway, at least.

During study hall, Dawn and I go to the office so Ms. Hernandez and Dr. Grayling can fill me in on details about the fundraiser.

"Emelyn!" Dr. Grayling says, waving us into the conference room. "Exciting things in the works, yes?"

Since I don't exactly know what's in the works, I look over at Ms. Hernandez for a cue.

"This is very exciting, Emmie," she says, smiling. "How did I not know you were working on earning yourself a new chair?"

They lay it out for me. The fundraiser will be in two weeks. Basically, the same fall carnival the junior high has every year, with an extra raffle that people can donate things for. All the money from the carnival and raffle will go toward buying my chair. Once I tell them how much I've already saved for it, the amount left to raise actually doesn't feel overwhelming.

It's all a bit surreal. Like something you talk about, daydream about, but never actually expect to become real. My brain is racing ahead of me, imagining what it will feel like to finally have a high-tech chair built for flying down inclines and hurtling over jumps.

It's going to feel like *freedom*, that's what.

Then Dr. Grayling adds, "And of course, there will be a media push beforehand. To generate public interest and whatnot."

"Media push?" I repeat. I hope that doesn't mean what it sounds like.

But it does.

The school has already reached out to the local news stations, I learn. I seriously wish they hadn't done that without asking me first. Or Dad, at least, and I think he'd have mentioned something like that.

"It'll be fantastic publicity." Dr. Grayling leans forward, talking a little faster, excited. "Wonderful optics for the school, a worthy cause. I'd call it a win-win."

I look at Ms. Hernandez. She's nodding and smiling like Dr. Grayling just said the weather forecast guarantees a week of perfect beach days. She and my mom may not have always agreed on exactly what was best for me when it came to services at school, but I know she's always been basically in my corner on most things.

"Okay," I tell them. "Sounds cool. I'll fill Dad in."

"Perfect." Dr. Grayling beams.

Soon Dawn and I are headed back up the hall to catch the tail end of my study period. "What do you think?" Dawn asks. She's clearly excited, and I remember she was the one who got all this started in the first place.

"It's wild," I admit. "And . . . thanks. How's your

mom doing?" I ask as an afterthought. "She and my grandma go to church together."

She lights up at my interest and shares a bit about her mom's most recent health problems. It sounds like she's got lots. I try my best to listen, but my mind keeps wandering back to last night, when AK_SalmonGranny asked if I hadn't been doing fine raising the money myself.

Now that I think more about it, she's dead right. I was actually doing great.

That realization gnaws a tiny hole in my excitement over everything that's happened today. Weirdly, it makes me think about fishing with Dad down at Nelson's pond, and how the best-tasting fish always seem to be the ones that are hardest to land. Those crafty fighters that take all you've got to reel in.

Somehow, those fish always taste so much better than one that's already caught and filleted. Or one someone randomly hands you when you weren't even all that hungry.

22

An Even Better Idea

Ale's totally exaggerating about me and Devontae playing one-on-one *every* single morning before school. Tina and Logan joined us at least once. And I didn't even drive over Logan's toes or anything. *Thinking* about doing it doesn't count.

Besides, we've got to brainstorm some more for our project, don't we? Even though Devontae's horse has invited me back to visit, that doesn't mean we should waste perfectly good time in the morning. Plus, it's way easier to talk without feeling nervous when we're passing the ball back and forth and looking at the basket most of the time.

So we play. Instead of HORSE, we shout out names and facts about the people we're choosing for our project as we try and outshoot each other.

"Dr. Ronald McNair. First Black astronaut. Walked

into a segregated library when he was nine years old, ended up leaving with a book to borrow. Died 1986 in the *Challenger* explosion."

"Katherine Beattie. One of the top WCMX riders in the world. From La Cañada Flintridge, California. First person with cerebral palsy to land a wheelchair backflip."

And so on. It's sort of fun, like we're not even working on our assignment.

One morning, Mr. Singletary comes over to join us. "How're the chair plans coming, Emmie?" He fakes, then swipes the ball from Devontae and runs in for a perfect layup.

"Lucky shot," Devontae jokes.

"Swap those boots for a pair of kicks sometime, and we'll see," Mr. Singletary fires back.

"The gear doesn't make the athlete," Devontae counters with a grin.

Dr. Grayling has been turning up at the gym door again this week, but now he actually comes in and sits in the bleachers sometimes. Once or twice, he even clapped when I made a basket. He still frowns when I pop a wheelie, but I make sure Mr. Singletary or Devontae stand behind me so he's got no real reason to fuss.

Just like with Dawn, I feel weirdly pressured to

be on best behavior around him, what with this fund-raiser in the works. It's a week away, which seems awfully fast.

Dad's home Saturday, which hasn't happened in a while. I know he's got some jobs lined up out in his shop, so I offer to help him. We have most of our best talks while we're turning wrenches anyway, and I want his input on a few of the final chair specs before I finalize the order form. But when I suggest going out there together, he shakes his head.

"Not today, Emms. I don't have anything interesting lined up at the moment."

"Then where are we going to catch the inspiration to finish customizing this chair?" I joke.

Dad looks troubled for a second. Then his face brightens.

"You want inspiration? I'll do you one better," he says with a little smile. "Grab your helmet and pads. And your water bottle. Be right back—need to run to the shop for a sec."

Since I'm right near the key hook, I start to grab the ring with the shop key on it to toss over to him, but it's not hanging in its usual place.

"I got it," Dad says, holding it up. "Be right back."

He comes back with his own helmet and pads crammed into a bag and his skateboard over one shoulder. I can't even remember the last time I saw him get on that.

When I realize what he's got in mind, I grin.

Dad's right. His idea is way better.

We load the truck and drive the hour and a half to Columbia, which has the nearest skate park. It's also where my doctor, therapists, orthotist, and wheelchair guy all have their offices. Other than that, we don't get out here much.

But today we just ride.

The park's almost empty, so we have the smooth concrete bowls, the grind bars and steps and kickers mostly to ourselves. Dad heads straight for the biggest bowl and does a perfect drop-in. For a few minutes, I'm happy to watch him fly back and forth. Dropping in, getting low, then shooting back up into a perfect kick turn at each lip.

I'd almost forgotten how good he is—and not only for an old guy. He rides that board like it's part of him. I recognize that *in the zone* look on his face, because I know I get it, too.

Of course, watching only lasts a few minutes. Then Dad rolls his board off to one side and helps me practice dropping in at one of the smaller bowls. The first few times he insists on running down beside me but finally loosens up enough to wait for me at the bottom. I want to try the grind rails, too, but Dad nixes that.

"Let's wait until you have the right chair for that, Emms," he says. "You want the grind bar option on the new one, right? We tear up the undercarriage on your regular chair, it's still a few years before insurance will cover a new one."

Much as I hate it, he's right. Tearing up my regular chair skating could be tough to justify for insurance to pay for—that's partly why Dad's always done so many of my repairs himself.

"See," I tell Dad after I finally ace a few drop-ins without any help at all. "I can totally do this at home."

Dad's smile fades. "The ramp's not safe, Emmie." He bends down and adjusts his knee pad, so I can't see his face. "And we both know your regular chair isn't designed for this kind of thing. I haven't changed my mind. Here at the park, me with you, is one thing. Hauling yourself solo up a heap of cobbled-together metal is another."

Yeah, but how often do we ever get the chance to come to Columbia? How am I ever supposed to get better if I only get to practice a few times a year?

When I start to argue, Dad changes the subject.

"How about that new chair of yours? You still leaning toward those Q-Grip handrims?"

That's a way more fun debate, so we take a break and discuss exactly which specs should go on the chair until we've got it basically locked down. I fill out the order form, which I brought with us, and Dad double-checks it.

"Can you send it over to Brent's office from work on Monday?" I ask when we're done.

Dad looks confused for a second.

"So that he can make sure we're not missing anything?" I persist. Brent's my regular wheelchair guy, who I see every year or so for my everyday chair fittings and any rare repairs Dad can't handle. This new chair is coming from a custom place out of Texas, not through insurance, so we didn't make an appointment with him about it. I think he should still look it over, and I'm surprised Dad didn't think of it, too. Even if Mom was always the one who made my appointments.

"Oh," he says when I tell him. "Right. Of course. Good idea."

All in all, it's a perfect day, and by the time we head home, we're both pleasantly tired and more than ready for drive-through sundaes on our way out of town.

Halfway home, I toss out the question that's been

nibbling at me all week. "Do you think it's weird that the school is buying this chair for me?"

He's quiet for a long minute, eyes on the road, sucking a bit of hot fudge from his plastic spoon. He doesn't say what we're both thinking—that Mom probably wouldn't have been a huge fan of the idea. Like, at all.

Finally, he says, "Only you know how you feel on that, Emms."

And it's nice, I guess, that he trusts me to make the call on this. Part of me, though, still wishes he'd tell me what he really thinks.

I shouldn't have to figure all this out by myself.

23

Quite the Daredevil

The next Saturday is the fundraiser. Dad drops me and Ale off early, promising to come back in a few hours after he finishes the job he's got on a tight deadline.

The gym is decorated for fall, like they do for the carnival every year—but this time there's also a long table along the far wall, covered with things people donated to be raffled. Ms. Hernandez and Ale's aunt Rosaria are setting up a ticket station on a card table. Someone's taken the picture of my dream chair I gave the office on Monday and blown it up poster size. Now it hangs on the wall over the raffle table in full color, so big that the red and green swirls of the Poison Apple frame really pop.

Definitely the right color choice.

A huge sign stretched under the picture tells everyone to BUY A TICKET OR TEN—HELP US GET EMMIE ROLLING!!

"Like you aren't already?" Ale whispers in my ear, looking down at my wheels, and we both laugh.

Soon people stream through the doors, and I see a reporter I recognize from the local paper two towns over. That's not surprising, since it doesn't take much at all to be newsworthy in a county the size of ours.

Before long, the carnival is in full swing. The games are hopping, delicious junk food smells fill the gym, and raffle tickets start selling fast. I see Dr. Grayling moving through the crowd, shaking hands and looking way friendlier than he ever does at school.

Ale and I meet the rest of our friends, and we all race around between the game booths and food tables for a while. It's glorious to not have Dawn with me, since it's not a school day. I do see her across the gym, and she waves at me with her free hand. Her other hand is holding the arm of an older lady who must be her mom.

When we start feeling tired of the games and full of food, we check out the raffle table. People have donated quilts and blankets, gift baskets from local businesses, all sorts of Carolina- and Clemson- and

Francis Marion–themed gear. I take a closer look at a handmade blank scrapbook and see *Donated by Dawn Wanamaker* on the little printed card beside it.

Wow. I was totally wrong when I dismissed Dawn's scrapbooking hobby as boring. This book—beautiful, intricate, full of tiny, hand-cut decorations and fancy trim—is a little piece of art.

Devontae shows up later, since he had a riding lesson this morning. I first notice him at the little card-table ticket booth with his parents beside him. Devontae whispers something to his dad, who nods and pulls a wallet from his pocket. Then Devontae sees me behind him and quickly tells his parents goodbye.

"What I miss?" He slides smoothly in with the rest of us.

"Don't you know nothing ever starts until you turn up, Boots?" I joke.

Devontae nudges a black-and-gold snakeskin boot against my footrest—barely brushing the laces of my Converse. "Didn't want to say it. Shuri says hi, by the way."

I turn away fast so he won't catch me grinning like some fool.

The afternoon passes quickly. Dad shows up, then Pop-Pop and Nonny. Just about the whole town, seems like. Everyone's laughing and eating and having fun and buying tickets.

That reporter keeps taking pictures of me. From across the gym, or a few feet away. He even catches me with my mouth wide open to bite into a hot dog. I tell myself it's part of the regular, boring county news cycle. He's probably taking embarrassing, open-mouth pictures of everybody here. Maybe.

Toward the end of the day, Ale and I use the last of our money on the ring toss and win little stuffed animals—a purple bear for her and a polka-dot octopus for me. I pop a wheelie to celebrate.

"Careful, Emelyn," says a voice behind me. It's Dr. Grayling, with the reporter right beside him. "She's quite the daredevil," he tells the reporter. "Keeps us all on our toes, but we do admire her spunk. She sure has overcome a lot. Right, Emelyn?"

I don't know how to answer that, so I sort of shrug-nod. Then the reporter snaps a picture of Ale and me each holding our stuffed prizes and asks me a few questions. Including—of course—the same old one I always get: *What happened to your legs?*

Dr. Grayling looks at me like he wants to say something, but then the art teacher's voice comes over the loudspeaker, calling everyone to the raffle area. By the time the last prizes have been claimed, it's clear a lot of money has flowed in. A few minutes later, they finish counting it up, and Ms. Hernandez screams the final amount into the microphone.

It's definitely enough for the new chair.

Just like that. It's *done*. Half of me feels excited beyond belief.

The other half feels weirdly left out.

"Before we wrap up," Ms. Hernandez says, "I know Emmie is so grateful to everyone here for their generosity. We hope you will all join us back here at E. L. Pinckney two weeks from tomorrow to help us celebrate as we present the money to Emmie right here on that stage!"

She points to the very back of the gym and the low stage the school uses for music performances and plays.

Wait, what?

Ms. Hernandez continues. "Now I want to mention some *especially* generous donors here and now. Let's give it up for Walter and Danitra Washington—and family—and their positively blessed gift of two hundred dollars to this most *worthy* cause!"

Something about being called a *cause* rubs me wrong. Mom used to call talk like that inspiration overload.

Ms. Hernandez claps her hands, still holding the mike, and gets the crowd cheering. She points to Devontae's parents, sitting in the bleachers. The spotlight that suddenly shines in their faces catches them off guard, but Mr. Washington gulps the last of his cupcake and gives the crowd a little wave. Mrs. Washington quickly swipes a napkin at a few crumbs on his lips.

"Two hundred?" Ale whispers. "That's no joke!"

Devontae is with them, a plate of red velvet cake in his lap. He catches my eye and gives me a huge grin that would normally be impossible not to return.

I try to grin back. But suddenly all I can think about is Devontae's perfect house. His perfect horse. His who even knows how many pairs of fancy boots. About dinner at his house, sitting under that perfect glass ceiling fixture that threw rainbows on the walls and into my eyes, feeling so aware of the holes in my jeans and hoping like heck I wouldn't break one of their fancy, perfect plates.

I don't like that feeling at all.

24

No Big Thing

RURAL COMMUNITY RALLIES, RAISES OVER $2,500 TO FUND WHEELCHAIR DREAM

Charles Hubbard, Staff Reporter

(Lakeville, SC) This year the annual Lakeville Fall Carnival, always a community crowd-pleaser, had an extra-special twist. Staff and students at E. L. Pinckney Junior High School pulled together a special benefit raffle for one of their own—an inspirational young woman with dreams of a brand-new wheelchair.

"It was a wonderful event," said Dr. Bruce Grayling, school principal and organizer of the event. "It goes to show what a small community can do when it sets its mind to it. And a worthy cause like this always strikes a heartstring."

The worthy cause is Emelyn Ethrige, a seventh grader at E. L. Pinckney and longtime source of inspiration to her classmates and teachers. Born with spina bifida, Emelyn has tragically never been able to walk, but that doesn't stop the young dynamo from being an active part of her school and community.

"Once we realized the cost of the chair," said Dr. Grayling of the school's decision to help raise the funds for Emmie's dream, "it made sense to pull together for her." Prior to his career in school administration, Dr. Grayling was active in mission-based fundraising to help disadvantaged communities in South and Central America.

The community raffle brought in an impressive $2,678. At the carnival, Emelyn had fun with her friends, enjoyed the games, and seemed excited and grateful for everyone's efforts on her behalf.

"It's definitely overwhelming," she said, when asked how she felt about everyone's helping her reach her goal. Then, true to her spunky nature, she rushed off to rejoin her friends.

The E. L. Pinckney JHS family will present the money to Emelyn in a community ceremony at the school on Sunday, October 24, at 7:00 p.m.

The article's taped up on the wall beside the office on Monday morning. I'm not sure why I have the sudden urge to peel it off, make it into an airplane, and aim it at the trash can.

Maybe I feel like I've missed a beat somewhere. All this time, Dr. Grayling has been so focused on all the things he thinks I *shouldn't* do. Watching me in the halls and in the gym, frowning like me wanting to do my thing is his own personal headache. Now he's suddenly head of the Emmie Cheerleading Squad. Leading the charge for a new set of wheels. Talking about it to people from the news. Something doesn't make sense.

Then there's the article itself. All those same old words like *inspirational* and *tragically* and *grateful* that everyone seems to assume wouldn't bug me . . . but they do.

It's like being stuck under a microscope.

In a wheelchair. Like some worm in a bait bucket.

I ride *on* wheels. Not *in* them.

Maybe it would be easier to explain if I was better with words.

Everybody's so excited, though. Even my friends.

Especially my friends, actually. And I don't know how to say any of those doubtful thoughts out loud without sounding like a jerk. I know how hard Ale and Tina worked on posters and social media for the fundraiser. Markus and Zeke and Devontae did a lot, getting donations to be raffled and helping decorate the gym. Lots of other people pitched in, too.

There's also the fact that Ale's still only halfway to saving enough for that hive she wants so much while I just sort of shot to the finish line without even earning it. I can't exactly *complain* to her about it.

So I try to smile and act super happy to everyone who comes up to me.

I manage all right for most of the morning. Then, before lunch, I stop to use the teachers' bathroom, the one that's big enough for my chair and opens right off the main hallway. I'm taking longer than I need to, getting a break from everyone coming up to me to talk about the raffle and the money. As I'm washing my hands, I hear a couple teachers stop in the hall outside and start talking to Dawn, who is waiting for me.

"Such an inspiring event, Miss Wanamaker," someone says. It sounds like Ms. Jiga, my study-hall teacher. "Once our Emmie gets a speedy new wheelchair, your job will only get harder, won't it?"

She won't have a job then, I remind myself. My new wheels will show everyone I don't need extra help.

It shouldn't sting so much, the laugh they all share.

Then another voice chimes in. "What's with the little romance brewing between her and Devontae

Washington? Has somebody got herself a bit of a crush?"

My head snaps up. Is it that obvious? Why on earth would teachers have anything to say about that, anyhow? I turn the water off slowly, so I can hear them better.

Dawn chuckles. "Cute as can be, aren't they? He's such a sweet young man—and such a generous gift from his family, wasn't it? I don't think it's any big thing, though."

I feel my face go hot. I know what she's not saying and what the rest of them are now all mm-*hmm*ing about. As much as I try not to let my mind go there, that makes me think about that two-hundred-dollar check Devontae's dad scratched at the raffle like it was pocket change.

I try to ignore it. I do. But it's too late. Somewhere deep down inside me, a hard little seed of doubt bursts into bloom.

It's still bothering me that evening. It's a school night for Dad, so he isn't here to talk to. I almost call Ale, but I'm afraid if I get talking, I might accidentally slip up and say something ungrateful-sounding about the fundraiser.

I decide maybe AK_SalmonGranny would be a safe bet. She's a million miles away in Alaska, so even if she thinks I'm an ungrateful jerk for having all these feelings, at least I won't see her disapproval in person. Plus, something tells me she might not think I'm being unreasonable. More and more, I wonder what she might have to say about a whole lot of things.

I grab the laptop off the coffee table and bring it to my desk. When I open it up, I see Dad's left his email open, logged into his inbox. I'm about to close it out when I notice the subject on the newest message.

FINAL NOTIFICATION: WITHDRAWAL/FAIL DEADLINE

My hand freezes, mid-click. The message is from the night school where Dad's taking his classes. I know I shouldn't read his message, but I can't stop myself.

Dear Student:

This notice is to inform you that you have reached the maximum allowed number of absences for the following course: ADT A296. Additional absences and/or the non-submission of pending missed coursework will result in a grade of F/Fail unless extenuating circumstances are immediately identified and discussed with your academic adviser and/or

program director. Please contact your adviser
immediately to address this matter.

Sincerely,
Department of Academic Affairs

I reread it about ten times, trying to make it mean
something other than what it does. Then I close out the
page, feeling gut-punched. If Dad hasn't been going
to class, then what has he been doing? *Why* hasn't he
been going to class?

Dad going back to school was something Mom
always wanted him to do. School was tough for him the
first time around, and when he decided to be a mechanic,
he did it through an apprenticeship program that paid
for all his certifications and training. Mom's point was
that if he actually went through a program and got a
two-year degree, then he could have way more options,
like teaching in a program himself one day.

Your body won't hold up forever, I remember her
telling Dad more than once, especially on days when
he'd come home with a tweaked back or a wrenched
shoulder from a heavy job or an accident at work.
*Getting a plan B on deck would give this family a few
more options.*

Like so many things, Mom was the driving force
behind a big idea, but Dad jumped on board, signing up

for two night classes a semester. Mom picked up more work hours to make ends meet and helped with papers when he had to write them . . . until the accident.

After that, everything got harder. Dad dropped down to one class a semester and worked full-time on top of that. I took on more responsibility at home to help out. We've done okay.

Until now, I guess. I turn off the laptop and stare at the black screen, trying to understand why he would have just stopped going to class. Without telling me.

More and more, it feels like Dad's second-guessing me. Or, when he does remember what I can do and how much fun we used to have doing everything together, suddenly catching himself and cutting it all back off. Like how he took me to the skate park but still won't let me actually get up on our own ramp to practice. Or how the key to the shop still hasn't reappeared on its hook by the door. Is he keeping the door locked on purpose? To keep me from . . . what? Bonking myself on the head with a lug wrench? Sending myself up one of the hydraulic lifts?

I'm not a little kid, dang it.

The longer I think about it, the madder I feel.

We're supposed to be a *team*. I'm holding up my end of the deal. Keeping dinner made, laundry done. Dealing with the whole aide-at-school thing all on my own so I don't give Dad one more thing to worry over.

Heck, I'm holding up *more* than my end of the deal here lately.

So why the heck can't he?

25

Rules Don't Change

I'm supposed to make a *speech*.

Just thinking about it makes me want to barf.

It would be so much simpler if the school could just send a check to my dad, or transfer money into a bank account, or send it directly to the wheelchair company when it's time to place my order. No, they want to *present* it to me. At school. Onstage. In front of the whole town. With newspeople. Cameras.

What a nightmare.

"God, I'm glad it's not me," Tina says with a shiver. We're all gathered around the lunch table on Tuesday, me trying not to think about it while everybody else can't seem to talk about much else. Dawn's sitting two tables away, since there's no room for her at ours with Logan here, so we can talk openly for a change.

"I mean, public speaking terrifies me!" she adds when I don't reply.

"Not helpful," I tell her.

"What are you going to say?" she persists.

I have no clue.

Logan, who's sitting next to Tina, throws in his two cents. "How come they're doing a ceremony only for the money?" he asks. "Will they do it again when you actually get the chair? So you can show it to everyone?"

Ale tosses him an annoyed look, then goes right back to the bee book she's been studying frantically since last week. She's been a bit quiet the last day or so, probably getting extra test jitters.

"Don't give them any ideas," I grumble, tearing a bite off my soggy pizza and trying to think of anything else to talk about. "Wish I knew why they want me to do all this nonsense."

Tina chews on her straw, thinking. "It actually seems on brand for Fish," she says. "My mom says he was always into some mission trip or another—loves helping the needy and all."

"I'm not needy!" I point out. "Besides, what's that have to do with me making some speech?"

Devontae winks at me across the table. "Not stressing over this, are you? I've never known you to be short on a comeback when you need one."

Easy for him to say. Besides, a quick zinger is nothing like an entire speech. I finish gulping down my lunch, trying not to think about how torn I still feel about his parents donating that much money to the . . . *cause*. It was incredibly generous . . . but I'm also starting to wonder if Devontae would even understand why I feel so edgy if I told him.

"Just itchy, I guess," I say finally. "Been too long since I cut loose a bit."

To make my point, I pop a quick wheelie and hold it. When I make it a full minute without even having to grab the table, I get even fancier and take one hand off my rims.

Then someone lifts my handgrips from behind, pushing my front wheels down. "Wheels on the ground, Ms. Ethrige."

I spin around. It's Dr. Grayling, of course, fun-killer that he is.

"Don't want any busted heads before next Sunday, do we?"

I bite back a rude answer. *Twelve more days*, I remind myself. Out loud I say lightly, "Guess I can hold off 'til the new wheels arrive."

He chuckles, like I'm oh so cute. "That will be nice, won't it?" he says. Then he even pats my chair like it's his pet poodle. "Rules don't change because we get new toys, though, now do they?" Before I can ask what that's supposed to mean, he heads across the cafeteria to annoy someone else.

My face burns. I turn back to my friends, who thankfully don't make a big deal over it, though I see Tina poke Logan hard in the side to keep him quiet.

I break for the door ten minutes before the bell, Dawn trailing after me. When I tell her I'm meeting Devontae in the library during study hall for our project, she gets a knowing grin.

"Isn't that nice," she says, and I get a stabby, annoyed feeling. I'm not sure who I'm even annoyed at right now. Fish? Dawn? Devontae? The whole school?

Either way, I just shove my wheels hard and roll faster so I don't have to think too hard about it.

When we settle down to work on our project, I can't focus. Dawn's up front talking to the librarian. She's gotten a little better about that—hanging back at the edges of a room instead of right up in my space all the time.

Still, all I want to do is move. Somewhere. *Anywhere.*

I do a crummy job of hiding it, because soon Devontae leans back in his chair and folds his arms over his red-embroidered Western shirt. "No pressure here," he says, "but we do need to get this nailed down—I wasn't joking that I only get to do rodeo if my grades stay up. I can tell your mind's roaming."

"No . . . yes . . . I know," I say. *Sort of had bigger things on my mind here lately*, I don't add. "I'm sorry. It's . . . I got a lot on my plate with everything coming up."

He nods. "I get that. You got to be excited as all get-out. I know how I felt when I finally got that new Chilean saddle I wanted so long."

Yeah. Not really the same thing.

For a minute, I think Devontae's going to let it go, but then he looks at me harder. "Is it just me," he says slowly, "or are you not excited about all this?"

I can tell he's confused why I wouldn't be. Just like he was so fence-post dense about those rodeo bathrooms that I had to spell it all out for him. I know he's not doing it on purpose, but I feel myself start to get a little annoyed.

"I . . . yeah." I sigh. "I sort of feel like I'm in a fishbowl since all this got started. It kind of happened before I even knew it was going to."

Devontae still looks confused. "Amazing, though. Everyone pulling together to help."

"That's just it," I say. "Everyone is so sure they're helping, but I was doing fine on my own before they got all up in it." I think about my wall chart, the red marker line, stalled out right over halfway since everything got put into motion.

I realize how much I miss filling in those lines each time I earned a bit more toward my goal. More than anything, I wish someone had thought to *ask* me if I needed help before going ahead and planning it all out.

Devontae's never seen my wall chart, and I'm bad at explaining, because I can tell he doesn't understand—and I *really* want him, of all people, to get it. I push back from the table and wheel back and forth a few times, trying to clear my head.

"Hey." Now Devontae looks a little worried. "Don't go stressing over it." He puts out a hand like he wants me to slow down, only his fingers don't land on my armrest. They land on my left rear wheel. Or, rather, on the hand that's gripping my left rear wheel.

My chair stops cold. My heart thuds like an air chisel against my ribs. Is his hand the one that feels like it's on fire? Or mine?

We stare at each other for a few supercharged seconds. If it was a mistake, he sure isn't rushing to move his hand. Part of me—the part that isn't irritated as all get-out—wants so, so badly to flip my wrist and let my fingers lace through his.

Instead, I yank my hand away like his is radioactive.

"I don't need your pity." The words come out sharper than I meant them, and he blinks a few times, looking stung. Part of me wants to cram the words back into my mouth—another part is so relieved to have actually said that out loud.

Part of me wants to say it to *everyone*.

The confused look on Devontae's face morphs into an offended one.

He lifts both hands palm out, like he's putting some distance between us.

"Is that what it was?" His voice is low, tight. "Glad you cleared that up for me, Emmie. Won't make that mistake again—let me get out of your way. Maybe I should go ahead and plan on doing the whole project myself while I'm at it."

The way he says my name isn't like when we were in his barn brushing Shuri. Now it's like he's talking to someone he just met. Or someone he thought he knew, but didn't.

Whatever. I don't care.

He starts to gather his things, but no way I'm letting him turn away first.

"Don't rush out." I throw my books into my bag so fast one almost bounces back at me. "I was just leaving."

Then, before he can get up—or see the way my stupid eyes go watery on me—I beat it out of there so fast I'm halfway down the hall before Dawn even makes it to the door.

26

Back in the Bag

I feel like everything's pushing down on me, making me itchy, desperate to *move*. On Thursday afternoon, I have to get back on the ramp. Ale sticks with me, helping boost me to the top and then back up again when I wipe out at the bottom. I'm too keyed up to focus, and I don't stick a single landing, but it feels so good to fly through the air and crash to the ground that I don't care. I keep readjusting my knee and elbow pads and wiping sand out of my eyes.

We do it at least two dozen times, until Ale's out of breath and I'm so sore and aching even I know I should probably give it a rest.

But I can't seem to stop.

So many things are spinning through my head. Mixing it up with Devontae when I'm not even exactly sure why I'm mad. This looming ceremony—just over a week away now—that I dread more each day. That email in Dad's inbox, saying he's got 'til the end of the week to get back into class or get kicked out.

The only way I can make all those voices shut up is with a whole lot of speed. And crash landings. I'll definitely have to do an extra-careful check of my legs tonight to make sure I haven't given myself any serious scrapes, but I'll worry about that later.

"Emmie," Ale says after my eighty-millionth wipe-out, "let's call it. We've both got homework." She looks at the sky, and I'm surprised to see it's nearly dark. "Plus, my certification test is in two days. I still need to go over—"

"Just a couple more." I pick grass out of a fresh scrape on my arm and tighten a knee pad. "Besides, you *know* you know all this boring stuff anyway."

Ale looks betrayed, and I realize I just called her biggest passion boring.

"Sure," she says tightly. "My interests mean nothing, but yours are important."

"What's that supposed to mean?"

"Sometimes I feel like what *you* like matters more than what I do. Or we do what you like more."

"That's ridiculous," I say, trying to ignore a little voice in my head that says maybe I have been a bit obsessive lately. Then I realize that Ale's legit mad.

"Emmie, make up your mind for once! What do you

even want? Do you want this new chair, or don't you? Do you want to do things we both like, or only what matters to you?"

I didn't know she felt that way.

"I know it's not your fault." Ale's face looks caught halfway between unhappy and guilty.

"What's not my fault?"

"It's just . . . how many more hours have we spent out here, me helping you up this ramp? Compared to how often you come help with my bees?"

That stings. "I'm afraid of the bees," I remind her.

"And sometimes I'm afraid you're going to kill yourself on this raggedy, rickety ramp!" she all but shouts.

"You're not the only one, Alejandra."

We both whip around. My dad is standing about a dozen feet away. His ball cap is pulled low over his eyes, arms folded so tight his muscles pop out under his tattoos.

"I think it's time for you to head home," he tells her quietly. Ale runs down the path between our places without even saying goodbye.

When she's gone, Dad stares hard at my scrapes and grass-caked pads. I'm about to come up with a good excuse, when suddenly he flat-out explodes.

"*What* have I told you? *How* many times?"

There's actual rage in his voice, which shocks me. I

try to calm him down, to laugh it off like usual, but he's good and ticked.

"I'm not sure"—his voice drops to a growl—"when you got it into your head that rules don't apply to you. That needs to change. You need to remember we're supposed to be a team. Now. Get inside."

I start to protest, but he spins around and stalks off to unlock the shop. Seeing him turn that key—locking me out *again*—floods me with sudden rage. *I'm* the one not being a team player here?

I shove my handrims hard and go after him, ready for a fight.

"When did you get so scared?" I shout.

He flinches, hand frozen on the doorknob.

"Oh, I don't know, Emelyn," he says in an awful, choked voice. "Maybe about two years ago when a car spun off the road, and suddenly *everything* was on me."

My breath stops. "Dad—" I start, thinking maybe I've gone too far.

His hand grips the knob so hard veins pop out. "I . . . I don't . . ." He shakes his head like it's filled with sand. "I *can't* do it all. Not like she could."

I suddenly think of all the things Mom always handled. My appointments. School clothes, permission slips, birthday parties. IEP meetings and basically fighting all my battles for me.

"You do good," I say quickly, because he does. I know how hard he works to take care of us, to keep things running. To keep our whole little testudo from falling apart.

Dad barely hears me. "It's not enough." He whispers it under his breath like he's telling himself a story. "It's never going to be enough."

My fingers tighten on my rims. "What's *that* supposed to mean?"

The ice in my voice finally gets Dad's attention. "Your mom wanted *so* many things, Emmie. For you— for us. She could always see the way to them so much clearer than me. I could work toward anything if she laid the groundwork, could tell me which way to pull. But now . . ."

I start to tell him it's okay, that we'll keep working together, no problem. Then he whispers something I know I'm not supposed to hear.

"Sometimes . . . I just *really* miss being *me*."

Dad's words hit hard, as if he slapped me. Which he would never, ever do, but it feels like what he says digs right down to my bones.

My shock must show, because Dad stops and stares at me. "Emms, *wait*," he says quickly, moving toward me. "I didn't mean that."

But that's the thing about letting the cat out of the

bag. You can't just wrestle it back in again. His words hang between us, cold and horribly honest.

"Sorry if I've been *inconvenient*." The words taste ugly in my mouth as I let them fly free. "You think Mom would have thought giving up was the way to get anywhere?"

His face turns to stone. "What did you say?"

Every sensible brain cell I have left screams at me to shut it, but I can't stop. "How is up and quitting on your class being a *team*? Were you even going to tell me, or did you think I wouldn't notice? That I'm some clueless little kid?"

For one awful moment, I think Dad's going to put his fist through the door. He shoves it open and goes inside, but reappears fast, carrying a sledgehammer and a pair of snips.

"*Do* you?" I persist. "You *know* I can work on cars. You *know* I can ride down ramps. You're the one who taught me! *What happened?*"

"Get. Inside. *Now.*"

He's never talked to me this way. Not even close. Fear floods me, and my stomach tries to claw its way up my throat.

I go. I spin around and fly across the path and up the ramp to the house as fast as I can go. Not quite fast enough to get there before I hear Dad's sledge slam into one of the vertical supports of the ramp he built.

Even though I knew deep down what he was about to do, that first hollow crunch of collapsing metal takes my heart down right alongside it.

At least I make it inside—just barely—before I start crying.

27

The Divine Right

I haven't talked to Dad.

I haven't texted Devontae to apologize.

Ale's beekeeping test was yesterday, but I haven't had the guts to message her and see how it went.

I *definitely* don't spend way too much time pointlessly staring at the raw spot in the field where the ramp used to sit.

School on Friday was a blur. Ale looked away every time I tried to catch her eye, and I used up half my headspace making sure not to cross paths with Devontae in the hallways.

On the bright side, having half my friends angry at me made it way easier to avoid talking to people. It took everything I had to get myself from class to class and out the door at the end of the day.

When Nonny stopped by the house this afternoon and handed me a folded-up stack of money,

I didn't resist. Not even when she told me it was to buy a "suitable dress" for the check-presenting ceremony.

I forced a smile, told her thanks, and took it.

After she left, I stared at the money in my hand. Logically, I know Nonny did it to be nice, but it felt like I'd just locked myself up and tossed away the key. Like I was going to this thing for real.

One more thing out of my control.

If that wasn't enough, another news person turned up Monday morning—this one from a TV station almost an hour away—wanting to get some footage of me—or, more to the point, of me and my wheels. She posed me in front of the school beside the Swamp Fox statue. Then she clipped a microphone onto my shirt and asked me, "How does it feel to be such an inspiration?" and "What would you like to say to everyone who donated the money to get you a new chair?"

She listened politely enough as I told her how I'd raised half the money myself before anyone else even knew about it. Dr. Grayling made sure she got a shot of him holding the front door for me on the way back inside and a bunch of Dawn handing me things or walking beside me in the hallway. I remembered what Tina's mom said about him being *all about helping the needy* . . . and felt the sudden, irrational urge to accidentally let the door slam on his hand.

Then, right before the reporter packed up her things, she asked Dawn if I had "any hope of ever being able to walk one day?"

To Dawn's credit, she just nodded toward me. "She's right there, you know." Then we both watched the lady fumble and blush, which was kind of nice.

It was all so painful it bordered on hilarious, and I started to head off to find Ale as soon as I escaped so we could laugh-rant about it. Then I remembered we weren't talking, and that warm, wanting-to-laugh feeling shriveled up into something cold and sad.

So yeah. Everything's basically in the toilet. The stinking, non-accessible toilet.

In six days, I'm getting on a stage in front of the whole school—probably the whole town—so they can hand me a check that's honestly as much about them as me. I wanted that chair—more than anything.

Now I'm realizing I didn't want it like this.

But the money is raised. The ceremony is planned. Too late to do anything but show up and look *grateful* for the people and the cameras. And *inspirational*.

I'd bet anything someone's going to tell me they'll have their church pray for me.

Then, after I flail through all that mess, I'm finally going to have that chair I came so close to earning all by myself. The chair that was supposed to change everything.

But deep in the whipped-up whirl of my thoughts, a nasty little suspicion is bubbling. A creeping, crawling feeling that it's not going to make one damn bit of difference at school.

Electric Grape. Poison Apple. Arctic Blast.

Who even flipping cares?

I feel so stupid for believing a frame color or killer suspension would ever matter. That wheelchair could be made of enchanted metal, with goblin-forged wheels and handrims glazed with fairy dust and unicorn tears. Wouldn't matter.

Wouldn't make the front door—or any other door— at E. L. Pinckney magically turn automatic. Wouldn't fix that stupid-steep, splintery ramp or the cramped bathroom stalls.

Won't make people look at me and actually see *me* before they see my wheels.

Won't change the fact that I'm just some redneck kid out in the middle of South Carolina, dreaming of something so stinking far away—in *every* way—that maybe it's foolish to even let myself dare.

It wouldn't bring back my ramp—the *one* place I had where I could actually practice.

Everything is rushing at me like a freight train. I almost break down and talk to Dad, but he's stayed gone even more than usual since our showdown. I woke up early on Saturday morning to the *clank-clank* of the trailer being hooked to his truck—then the crash and scrape of twisted metal as he hurled the broken pieces of the ramp onto it to be hauled off to the scrapyard.

He hasn't come in from the shop before I've gone to bed one single night since our blowup.

In the mornings, I stare out the truck window and count mailboxes as we ride silently past houses and trailers and wide-open fields to school. Dad chugs coffee like he's drinking magic elixir and stares blearily at the road, gripping the wheel like he's trying not to fall off the edge of a cliff.

Nobody ever tells you that one day you'll wake up and realize your parents are just flailing along, faking it like everybody else. If they're even still here at all.

All my life, I had two heroes. I thought I'd *always* have two heroes. But then I lost one two years ago, and now the one I have left is melting away a little more each day.

It hurts to even look at my dad right now.

So I don't.

Later that afternoon, the desperation to talk to someone reaches a breaking point, and I call Pop-Pop to ask for a ride and not tell Nonny where he's going.

"How long you want me to stay gone, Biscuit?" he asks once we arrive. I tell him about an hour, and he gives me a hug before he gets back into his car.

"Take as long as you need," he says. "Might take more time than you think. Or less."

With that confusing advice, Pop-Pop pulls away, and I roll up the path under the iron HOLY CROSS arch. For the first time I can remember, I don't even feel tempted by all the smooth, crisscrossing walkways or the low, hoppable steps tucked around the cemetery.

Mom's grave looks as peaceful as ever. The headstone is covered with little golden patches from the sun shining through the trees. Nonny and Dad must not have completely stomped the new flowers during their epic face-off, because I see blossoms—purple and yellow—starting to uncurl. They were Mom's favorite colors, I remember.

I guess Nonny must remember that, too.

People in movies always have these deep, meaningful

talks—or a surprise encounter with zombies—when they visit a cemetery. But I'm just not much good at one-sided conversations. I tried at first, but it never felt like I was talking to anyone but myself.

Still, I'm about out of other options.

So I push myself over the grass and brace my rear wheels against the back of Mom's headstone. Then I flip the brakes on and slide from my chair to lie on the cool, soft grass. I stare up at the oak leaves and autumn sunlight and pale blue Carolina sky and try to think of what the heck to say.

"It's all gone to hell, Mom" is what I come up with.

Okay, maybe not ideal cemetery language. AK_SalmonGranny must be rubbing off on me. I try to think what I'd tell Mom if she were lying beside me. Knowing her, she'd be pointing out clouds and telling me what states or countries they look like to her.

"I didn't know it was going to be so hard," I finally say.

What do I even mean? Dad and me, trying to make it all work without her and sometimes feeling like we're barely hanging on. Me, getting older and slowly realizing how much Mom had always been fighting my corner all those years without my ever fully knowing.

Maybe, most of all, coming face-to-face with the

awful truth that my first and best buffer against the whole stinking world isn't ever coming back. And that Dad—as much as he loves me and would work himself six feet under for me—can't ever be *everything* Mom was.

That maybe I haven't been totally fair expecting him to be.

I blink hard and stare at the clouds some more. I think I see one that looks like Denmark, but I'll have to double-check. I haven't paid much attention to geography since Mom . . .

Then some of Mom's words drift through my memory, and I almost smile.

The Divine Right of the Bipedal. It was something Mom used to say now and then. Especially if she was frustrated or mad about someone trying to tell her not to expect too much from me, or that they didn't know "how she managed to cope with it all."

"The Divine Right of the Bipedal," she'd say, rolling her eyes like she'd heard the most dang-fool punchline ever. "Amazing how powerful that creed can make someone feel."

I guess I never truly got it when I was little, or maybe it seemed like a joke she'd say when she was annoyed. Now I think I do.

I think she meant the world's probably always going to be full of people who think they know how far I can go, what I should dream about.

What my family should—and shouldn't—want for me.

That they've got the right to say to my face that they could never handle being like me.

Or that I need to take whatever anyone offers me and best be grateful.

Like moving through life on legs instead of wheels somehow gave them the right.

Which is all such *crap*.

28

Ohh, Honey . . .

Talking with—well, *to*—Mom at Holy Cross left me with more questions than answers, which probably shouldn't feel surprising. I wish more than anything that I could just text Ale and tell her everything. But I don't even have it in me to try right now.

So, after arguing with myself whether it would be weird—and then deciding I don't care—later on Monday night, I send a message to AK_SalmonGranny. She might be the only person I know—sort of—who could actually *get* all the thoughts clogging my brain.

At least I hope so.

HalfpipeEmms: Hi. Not to be weird, but did you know how the chair thing was going to go down?

AK_SalmonGranny: There are no weird questions, dearie. There are, however, recipients of questions who can be a bit slow on the uptake . . .

HalfpipeEmms: ?

AK_SalmonGranny: Been filleting halibut since 6am

over here. Hard on the old brain cells after a few hours. On the old hands, too. Tell me what you mean. Small words.

HalfpipeEmms: Oh. Gotcha. I like fishing, too. I meant about my school raising money for my new wheelchair. You said hadn't I been doing fine on my own. I didn't get it at first, but I think I do now.

AK_SalmonGranny: Ah.

HalfpipeEmms: ?

AK_SalmonGranny: Well.

HalfpipeEmms: Sorry is this weird that I'm asking u?

AK_SalmonGranny: Not at all.

HalfpipeEmms: ???

AK_SalmonGranny: Okay, serious talk. I knew because people are people. For better or worse.

HalfpipeEmms: Did you have to have an aide at school when you were a kid? Or special ed?

AK_SalmonGranny: Interesting name, isn't it? Never could figure out what was so "special" about just giving every kid what they needed at school.

I'd never thought of it that way before.

AK_SalmonGranny: But to answer your question, no. Wasn't always a wheeled wonder, me. You?

HalfpipeEmms: Yep. Since forever.

AK_SalmonGranny: I see. Well, even if I had been, things used to be quite different on that front.

HalfpipeEmms: What do you mean?

AK_SalmonGranny: 504 Sit-In.

Does she mean 504 like my school plan? When I ask, her reply is super fast.

AK_SalmonGranny: Yes. The very same. I was there, in fact. Interesting times.

HalfpipeEmms: I'm confused.

AK_SalmonGranny: You should probably look it up. You young folks are good at that, right?

HalfpipeEmms: Okay

AK_SalmonGranny: No rush, I'll be here. Halibut's already in the oven.

I look it up.

What I find out shocks the heck out of me.

Those 504 plans I review with Ms. Hernandez every year—the ones that go on and on about my "reasonable and necessary accommodations" and always seem *so* boring and annoying? They weren't even a thing a few decades ago.

Not only that—if I'm reading right—less than fifty years ago, people who used wheels didn't necessarily go to school *at all*. At least not public school. Schools didn't have to let them in. Or give them any accommodations. That's what the 504 protests were all about.

People like funny, feisty AK_SalmonGranny.

People like all the other kids at my school who have disabilities.

People like *me*.

Fighting for the right to an education.

For the right to . . . be treated like *people*.

Seriously? It used to be legal—*common*—to not let some kids even come to regular school? Just because they used wheels or needed other kinds of help?

I think about all the kids at E. L. Pinckney who need help from teachers or aides to do certain things during the school day. Like Demarion, who holds a brush in his teeth and makes some of the coolest paintings I've ever seen. Or Tina, who takes all her tests in the resource room and sometimes records classes instead of writing notes because of her dyslexia. Would they all have just had to stay home? Not get to learn or make any friends?

Then I think about myself and what my life might have looked like if I'd been born before the 504 Sit-In. Or in a place where the laws still haven't changed.

It all feels like a gut punch.

How did I not ever know about this?

All this new information makes my head spin. But I'm still sort of stuck on all my other issues. So for now I file it away for later and tell AK_SalmonGranny about what's been going on. School, Dawn, Devontae, Ale, Dr. Grayling—everything. Then I ask her advice.

AK_SalmonGranny: Hoo-boy. Your school did it up in

style, didn't it? Up on the stage and everything. Sounds like somebody had a lot of fun planning that.

HalfpipeEmms: Yeah ☹

AK_SalmonGranny: Afraid I don't have many concrete answers. I don't doubt that everyone probably had good intentions. Sometimes that makes it harder.

I frown at the screen, wishing she'd just tell me what I'm supposed to do.

HalfpipeEmms: Well, can you tell me when all this gets easier?

AK_SalmonGranny: Explain.

HalfpipeEmms: How old were you? When all this life stuff made more sense?

Hitting send on that one feels good, like I've finally landed on the question that's been chewing at me all along. Her response takes a long time. Or maybe it only feels that way.

AK_SalmonGranny: Ohh, honey.

HalfpipeEmms: Like a long time???

AK_SalmonGranny: Like, never.

HalfpipeEmms: Never?

AK_SalmonGranny: Afraid so. Why do you think I compensate with snarky accessories?

HalfpipeEmms: What about boys? Will they always be this confusing?

AK_SalmonGranny: I don't know about boys, dear. But

relationships? Yes. They're about as simple as three tangled fishing lines.

HalfpipeEmms: Nooooo

AK_SalmonGranny: You wanted it straight, yes?

HalfpipeEmms: Um. Yeah?

AK_SalmonGranny: But you wanted a different answer.
I understand. None of this is easy. Adults learn to fake it a
little better—if they're lucky.

This is *so* not the answer I was hoping for.

Still, a tiny part of me feels good to hear all this
from someone else. To sort of give words to all the big,
scary, overwhelming things I've been trying to navigate with no GPS.

HalfpipeEmms: Okay. But what do I do RIGHT NOW?

AK_SalmonGranny: For me, it's doing whatever the
heck I feel like, whenever the heck I feel like doing it. But
I'm an old, crotchety lady who can do what I please. I don't
know what your answer is—but you're probably going to
have to speak up for yourself. And make things right with
your friend somehow.

I stare at the screen for a long time.

Seriously.

For all my fussing about wanting people to back off
and let me do my thing . . . right now I'd give anything
for someone to hand me an answer or two.

29

How **Not** to Help

The next day, I stay back when the bell rings and everyone rushes out of Mr. Milling's class. Dawn, who has to get her mom to another doctor's appointment, doesn't argue when Mr. Milling tells her she can go ahead. She grabs her jacket, tells us bye, and disappears. I wait at my desk until the rest of the class files out and try to pretend it's my imagination that Devontae took the long way around the classroom to avoid having to walk past me on his way to the door.

When the room is empty, Mr. Milling comes and perches on the desk next to mine.

"What can I do for you, Emmie?"

"I . . . wanted you to know it's not Devontae's fault we're behind on our project," I tell him. "He's been trying to get us going. We even got together a few times to work on it." I probably deserve a bad grade, honestly, but I don't want Devontae getting sidelined from rodeo because I haven't been able to keep focused on everything.

"And?"

"It's just . . . lots of things haven't gone so good here lately."

Mr. Milling nods, blowing out a breath and looking thoughtful. I wonder what all he's heard in the teacher breakroom. Now that I know for sure that some teachers have no problem gossiping about who might or might not like who, who knows what else he could know?

"You thinking about Sunday?" he finally says.

"Yeah."

Mr. Milling's quiet for a few seconds. "Anything I can do?"

I think about it. "I don't think so. But thanks." Then I suddenly have to ask. "You ever heard of the 504 Sit-In?"

His forehead scrunches up, and I'm half disappointed he doesn't know, but half pleased to have stumped a teacher as smart as him. I tell him what I read about yesterday, and he starts nodding like he's just remembered something. "Right, right," he says. "I did learn about that back in college. Did you know, the Black Panthers provided food for those protesters during the sit-in? Lot of brave, determined people working on that. They did it, too—got those laws changed."

"That was only, like, fifty years ago!" The words burst out of me, and it feels good to say it—how *wrong* that is—to someone else.

"Lot of things weren't all that long ago," he says, and now his face is stony. "Plenty still going on today." After a moment, he adds, "You know, Emmie, injustice can look like a lot of different things we don't always know how to recognize."

I must look as baffled as I feel, because he laughs and clarifies.

"I mean, I know what injustice looks like from inside my own skin—but I don't know what it looks like from your wheelchair. Or from countless other perspectives. We know what we know, and make mistakes about what we don't. That's why we keep talking to each other. Speaking up. Educating, and letting ourselves be educated. Only way we'll ever get anywhere."

"Even if I'm just a kid?" *Even if I'm just me?*

"Especially because of that." Mr. Milling glances at the bulletin board where he hangs students' papers and projects that are especially good. Then at the back wall, where he tapes up news stories about kids from different places who've gotten involved in their communities or become activists for human rights or the environment in cool ways. "We all need allies . . . and to *be* allies . . . and it's tough to be a good one.

Sometimes you've got to all but grab folks and shake them to show them how *not* to help. Not saying it's easy—lots of times it's flat-out infuriating. But it's important."

Then Mr. Milling checks his smartwatch and smiles. "On that note, how about I end the lecture you never asked for, let you get on with your day?" He hops off the desk. "I'll give you and Devontae an extra few days for your project outline, given all you've had going on. In the meantime, you think hard about what you want to say come Sunday."

I promise I will. When I head for the door, he starts to follow me out, then stops.

"So, you're okay on the ramp?" he asks, and I can see him trusting me to tell the truth.

"Yeah," I say. Then I pop a wheelie and hold it, one handed, testing to see if he'll tell me to stop. He raises his eyebrows, looking impressed. "It's a sorry excuse for a ramp," I can't help adding, "but I can do it myself."

"Okay, then." Mr. Milling goes to his desk and sits down. "See you tomorrow, Emmie."

The halls are mostly empty as I collect my things from my locker. As I'm about to slam it shut, Logan comes around the corner.

"Hey, Emmie!" he calls, and hurries over before I

can hide behind the door or close it quick and escape. I shove the last of my books into my bag, and one slips from my fingers and thumps to the floor.

"I *got* it," I say automatically, throwing up a hand to keep Logan away. Then I realize he hasn't moved toward me—or the book. He stands there with his hands in his pockets, looking like he wants to dive for it so bad it itches. But he doesn't.

A little surprised, I lean over and grab my book. Then—grudgingly—I give him a little nod, silently thanking him for staying out of my space.

Logan, being Logan, doesn't leave it at that. "Yeah," he says, like we're talking about the next basketball game. "Tina told me it isn't cool to try to help you if you haven't asked."

"Tina's right."

"Then Ale sort of cornered me at the stove in the home ec room and said it was basically my fault you got stuck with an aide."

Now Logan looks embarrassed, which I don't think I've ever seen before. I don't disagree—I never would have fallen on that ramp if he hadn't raced over and gone grabbing at my wheels. But, if I'm honest, it wasn't only him.

It was the steep, splintery ramp itself. The hot, pitchy sap that leaks out of that cheap wood on every sunny day. The sun flashing off Devontae's big old belt buckle.

And—I guess I should just admit it—my own constant need for speed that catches me up now and again. It was all of that, wrapped up into one sticky mess. I shrug and slam my locker, then we head down the hall together. When we're at the front doors, something occurs to me, and I can't resist.

"So, if Ale and Tina telling you not to help unless I ask was enough to convince you"—I pause; the thought takes shape in my head, clearer and clearer until I finally know how to put it into words—"why wasn't it enough when *I* told you?"

I swear, Logan looks as surprised as if I'd bopped him between the eyes. He actually stops walking for a second and blinks.

"I . . . I guess . . . I don't know. I'm sorry."

It's a Logan-honest answer, and still frustrating. But at least he's trying to learn. "Okay," I say. "Just so we're clear."

"We are."

Logan's silence after that lasts all of five seconds. "How long you and Devontae going to stay mad?" he asks, like a fight's something you can set a timer to.

"How am I supposed to know?" I sigh. "It's not

like baking red velvet cake." I dang sure don't let on anything foolish about all those bone-deep, irrational doubts that got hold of me about why Devontae was even spending time with me to start with.

Of course, Logan has something to say anyway.

"Well, I think you're both wasting a whole lot of time." Classic Logan Whitten. "Any fool can see y'all like each other."

I *don't* tell Logan a blessed thing more about Devontae and me. But that evening, in my room, I spend two hours roughing out a draft of an imaginary letter from Katherine Beattie to her mom, describing what it felt like to catch air for that first-ever backflip. It's no masterpiece, but it's a start.

After changing my mind about fifty times, I upload the file and send it to Devontae.

(7:46pm) HalfpipeEmms: Here's #1—KB. Thought maybe Shuri could look it over?

(7:52pm) HalfpipeEmms: You could tell her I think I've figured out what to do for the last one. I think she'll like it.

(8:34pm) HalfpipeEmms: Maybe she could work on Bill Pickett? Since he was so into horses and all . . .

(9:22pm) HalfpipeEmms: Do horses ever say things they wish they could take back? Maybe that's what that "straight from the horse's mouth" my Pop-Pop's always saying means.

(9:45pm) HalfpipeEmms: Anyway. Tell her she's not the only one.

(9:56pm) Broncs&Boots: Shuri says thanks. It's a start.

30

Wouldn't That Be Special?

On Wednesday morning, Dawn and me get called into Ms. Hernandez's office. I try to remember if I've done anything to get in trouble the past few days but can't think of anything. Mr. Singletary and Ms. Parsons are already inside, sitting down. So is Dr. Grayling. They want to talk about Sunday, surprise, surprise.

"Emelyn," Dr. Grayling starts off. He clap-rubs his hands together and smiles. "I've been talking with Ms. Hernandez and Ms. Parsons. They tell me you can actually walk!"

"What?" Dawn sounds excited. "I never knew that!"

"*No.* Not exactly." I glance at Ms. Hernandez, feeling a little betrayed. Yes, I can walk a tiny bit, mostly a few steps here and there at home, if I'm holding on to something. But it's never been—and it's never going to be—the main way I get around. Some of my muscles just aren't hooked up to the power source, so to speak. Which is why wheels have always made the most sense for me. I'm cool with that.

Everybody else should be, too.

"Why?" I ask.

Ms. Hernandez clears her throat, looking uncomfortable. "Here's the thing, Emmie," she says. "Mr. Singletary brought up the very good point that the stage we're using in the gym on Sunday doesn't have . . ."

Of course. They finally remembered about the steps.

"It's got stairs," I finish for her. Two short sets in front, two short sets in back, out of view of the audience and accessed from a rear door. I don't know why, but something about this all suddenly strikes me so funny, in a terrible, infuriating way.

Bringing me up onstage to give me some big presentation—helping the *needy* and all—and nobody stopped to think that the stage isn't wheelchair accessible?

I bust out laughing.

Everyone looks at me a little nervously, so I try to focus.

"Yeah, but not many," I say. "I can probably go up the back, if I use the railings and have someone pass the chair up."

"Ms. Hernandez mentioned that option," Dr. Grayling

says, clearly uninterested. "But I thought—*we* thought"—he waves his hand to include everyone and doesn't notice when they all look surprised—"wouldn't it be special if the audience could *see* you go up the stairs in front?"

"Special for who?" I burst out.

"Don't worry," he says quickly, maybe mistaking my irritation for fear. "Ms. Wanamaker could help you, be right there with you."

Dawn opens her mouth and then stops, looking at me uncertainly.

"Yeah . . ." I say quickly. "The back way would be easier. Mr. Singletary can pass up my chair. Or my dad."

"Sure can, Emmie," Mr. Singletary says. "Got you covered."

Ms. Parsons and Ms. Hernandez nod, like this makes sense.

Dr. Grayling leans back in his chair. "Well," he says, looking unsatisfied, "the choice is yours, I suppose. But it never hurts to consider the overall effect . . ."

His voice trails off, but suddenly I know exactly what he's not saying.

He's in help-the-needy mission mode. He wants me to put on a show.

For the audience, for the cameras. For all those

"media push" and "optics" things he's been going on about. *That's* what he wants.

Strangely enough, I actually think he believes he's doing me a favor here . . . and I don't know how to explain that he's not.

"*I* think," Ms. Parsons breaks in, "that what we all should be thinking about here . . . is what's best for Emmie. And I say that's whatever *she* wants."

"Exactly." Ms. Hernandez nods so hard her glasses slide down her nose.

"Agreed." Mr. Singletary folds his arms.

Dawn looks back and forth between everyone like it's a Carolina–Clemson playoff.

Dr. Grayling opens his mouth, then shuts it.

I finally find my voice. "I'll go up the back way, thanks. Unless y'all can get a ramp built by Sunday."

Okay, I probably didn't need to throw in that last bit. But having those three around me, looking ready to jump in if I need it, gives me the courage to say it anyway.

Even though they don't understand exactly why I don't feel so hot about all that's about to go down, I feel like they *want* to understand.

I still can't quite find the words to explain it, though, and I desperately wish I could.

31

Just Ask

I still don't know how to fix things with Ale. I'm sort of running low on words, but I hate this awful silence between us, and now I get that I've kind of been taking her for granted. I accuse Dad of getting tunnel vision sometimes, and here I'm not much better.

I need a peace offering.

So I set my alarm super early Thursday morning, grab two empty buckets from the garage, and spend an hour collecting pine cones beneath the two biggest trees in our yard. Ale usually collects the cones, since it takes me longer, what with getting my wheels across the bumpy, sandy ground and getting down low enough to grab the fallen ones. I use the reacher-grabber thingy I got from some therapist forever ago that's been stashed in my closet, which helps. Pinching up the cones without cracking them takes a bit of practice. It's boring, rhythmic work that doesn't let me move fast enough to avoid thinking.

Not my favorite headspace, but probably exactly what I need.

I stab at the cones, transfer them into the slowly filling buckets, and take stock of where I am. No closer to much of anything, other than maybe inching toward some kind of peace with Devontae. Still too early to tell, but at least we're sort of talking again.

At least *Shuri* still seems to want to talk to me. A little.

When I've got both buckets full, I hang them over my handgrips and roll carefully down the path to Ale's house, planning to leave them beside her porch. Her mom is in their yard, busting dance moves that make her long, dark ponytail whip around as she tosses feed to the hens. She yanks out her earbuds when she sees me.

"Hola, Emmie," she says, juggling the earbuds and phone, and waves me over before I can change my mind. Ale is nowhere in sight, so I join her and explain why I brought the cones. Then I ask how Ale's bee-keeping test went. She killed it, of course, which I already guessed. Ale's mom promises to give Ale the pine cones and sets the buckets on the porch, shooing off a few curious hens. Then, unexpectedly, she kneels down beside me.

"Don't be a stranger, mija." She squeezes me into a hug. "Arguments can be fixed."

My face gets hot, though I'm not sure whether it's embarrassment that she knows about our fight or jealousy that Ale has her mom to talk to about it. Maybe Ms. Che reads my mind, because she hugs me again, then pushes me back to arm's length, still holding my shoulders.

"Ale misses you," she says, "and you're not the only one who misses your mamá. She was my friend, too."

I'm surprised to see that Ms. Che's eyes, big and dark brown like Ale's, look teary. "All our hearts still hurt," she continues. "I know it's not the same, but you can talk about her with me anytime you want."

I suddenly remember fall evenings, in our yard or theirs, our families gathered around a firepit, making s'mores and roasting hot dogs and corn. My mom and Ale's, playing their guitars and laughing, everyone singing along as they plucked out songs.

It hurts to think about, but it helps, too. Knowing it's not only me who feels that hole. I hug her back, my eyes stinging. "Thanks."

"You got a mamá here, too," she says, sternly now. "All you need to do is *ask*, mija."

Just ask.

Speak up.

Why do I keep hearing that lately?

I don't know if it's the guitar music that blasted from Ale's mom's phone, or her surprising, sweet offer to be there if I need a "mamá." Either way, later that afternoon, something makes me go and dig through my parents' closet for Mom's old costumes.

I lay them carefully out on the bed, smoothing a tulle skirt here, an embroidered corset there. Mom loved dressing up so much, and some of the costumes she put together were impressive. When I turn out the light and leave, I have three of her dresses in my lap.

Then, after a lot of thought, I go back one more time. I dig farther into the closet, to the very back, until my fingers find the neck of her guitar.

When Dad gets in from the shop late in the evening, I'm in the living room, picking out chords on Mom's guitar with some help from YouTube. His eyes dart from Mom's dresses on the couch to her guitar in my hands, and his shoulders go rigid. I swallow hard and keep playing, ready to do battle if he tries to stop me. But he just drops into his chair, presses his fingers into his eyes, and listens to me play until I run out of chords, which doesn't take long.

When I set the guitar aside, he opens his eyes. "Time to talk?"

I shrug, both knowing we probably need to and dreading actually doing it.

"First off," Dad says, "I owe you an apology. Probably a couple years' worth."

It isn't the opener I expected, and all the defenses I've been gathering sort of melt away. I chew my lip, thinking. Finally, I say, "I'm not a little kid. You shouldn't hide things from me."

He sighs. "Actually, Emmie, you are. Hear me out," he adds, holding up his hands as I start to protest. "I know you're not a little kid in . . . a lot of ways. But in other ways, you *are*. Or, you should get to be. I'm supposed to be the one helping you with the big things. School." He bites his lip. "Loss. *Grief.* Not the other way around."

"It's okay," I start to say, but he shakes his head.

"No. It's not. And I'm sorry. I'm going to do better."

I think about the ramp, hauled off to the scrapyard in a trailer load of twisted junk. As angry as it makes me to think about it, I also feel sad for Dad, who I know loved that ramp, too. Maybe I'm saddest for the Dad I remember from before—my carefree partner in mischief.

"I guess after busting out a sledgehammer and snips, the only way left to go is up," I joke.

Dad looks surprised for a second, then chuckles. "Can't argue that," he admits. He stares at Mom's guitar for a long moment. Then he walks across the room, picks it up, and runs his fingers over the strings.

"Dear God," he says, and the pain in his voice reminds me how alone he looked that day at the Fairy Festival, standing behind the stage with tears on his face. "She was so proud when she brought this home."

"I want to learn to play it."

"I think we can manage that," he says. "You know, I can't even remember which painting this was. She loved so many." He touches the long-haired lady in the boat printed on the guitar. "Isn't that terrible? Your mom wanted so bad to go see it for real one day, and I can't even recollect the name of her favorite painting. Much less the museum where it is."

That does seem awfully sad, and I feel worse as I realize I can't remember, either.

Then, out of nowhere, a scrap of memory bubbles up. Words scrawled on the side of Mom's last coffee can.

Tate Fund!!! ☺ ☺ ☺

I grab Dad's phone and start searching combinations of *Tate* and *Lady in Boat*. It doesn't take long to find it.

The Lady of Shalott. 1888. John William Waterhouse. Tate Britain, London.

When I show Dad, he smiles. "Sounds about right," he says with a choky little laugh. "Of course it's not someplace sensible like Atlanta or Charlotte. Never had time to dream small, your mom."

She sure didn't. But Dad and I need to find our own dreams to work toward, too. Some of hers, yes, but I think we also need a few new ones. Just for us.

"Are you going back to class?" I ask. I don't want to mess up the fragile peace we're finding, but I need to know. Maybe part of me wants to know if this is something Dad honestly wants, or what Mom wanted for us all.

I look at him, afraid of the answer.

When Dad answers, he chooses his words carefully.

"I think so, Emms," he says. "But not quite yet. Got a few things need wrapping up first."

"What kind of things?" I know I sound suspicious, but who can blame me with all the bad surprises here lately? But Dad just hands Mom's guitar back to me, looking like his mind's already someplace else.

"You'll see" is all he'll say.

32

Pinch the Moon

I get edgier and edgier as Sunday approaches, which of course I can't hide. On Friday evening, Dad—who actually came in early today—gets tired of jumping back to avoid his toes being driven over and pulls me up short.

"Enough of this," he says. "You're wearing holes in the floor. Come on, Emms. Could use some help in the shop."

That sounds so good I don't stop to ask why he's suddenly changed his mind—either about stopping me from working out there, or now suddenly deciding to let me again. I throw my hair into a ponytail, pull on a ball cap, and follow him outside.

Dad's shop is way too big to belong beside a regular old place like ours—it could be a legit commercial one. He built it from the ground up and put in three entire work bays. Two of them are equipped with full lifts and everything else you need for a complete auto shop. He collected or traded for things for it over the years, and Mom used to joke that the shop was her biggest competition. When we go in and Dad flicks the lights on, at first I don't realize what I'm seeing.

When I finally get my jaw closed and look away from what's standing in the third bay, my eyes meet Dad's. He's got a smile on that I haven't seen in . . . well, a *long* time.

"Surprise?" he says softly.

The third work bay is filled with a real half-pipe, made of solid metal supports and a slick, sanded-wood surface that curves up on both sides into a perfect bowl. That's not all. Low, wide wooden steps run up along the side on one end. A solid railing with handgrips, wide enough for me to pull myself up while towing my chair. At the other end of the half-pipe is a landing pit, huge and perfect and filled with big chunks of foam.

Perfect for landing in without banging yourself up.

My eyes go blurry. "I thought you locked the door because you didn't want me helping you anymore."

"I know," Dad says. "I'm sorry about that—and for all the time you've been on your own at night while I've been working on this. Wanted to surprise you. Was trying to hold out until your new chair got here. Then I realized if I wanted to stop worrying about you totaling yourself, I needed to step it up a bit."

I stare at the perfect setup, and a thought slowly dawns.

"So, you never actually believed I couldn't . . . ?"

Dad pulls off his cap and runs a hand through his already messy hair. "Of *course not*, Emms," he says. "But that raggedy old ramp of mine wasn't safe. Probably not even for me to use anymore. I've had to get used to your mom not being around to reel me back here and there when I don't think about some of those things. Maybe I went too far the other way. But how could I believe you couldn't do it? I mean, whose kid are you?"

I immediately think of Dad at the skate park, flying over the curves on his board as easy as breathing.

"You know," I point out, "you could've just said something."

Dad laughs again, only this time it's more than a little choky. "Don't you know by now? This *is* how I say something."

I *do* know.

It's all so clear now.

Dad built this whole, beautiful setup for me. That's probably why he flunked his class, why I haven't seen him for weeks. One-track Dad, charging forward toward one most important thing and accidentally forgetting everything else in the process.

All to show me what he can't ever quite say. That he absolutely believes in me.

Dad pulls it together, barely. "I never told you why I built the shop so big, did I?"

"Yeah?"

"Plain old gut-wrenching fear. I'd just found out your mom and I were expecting you, was flat-out terrified. Was practically still a kid myself, no idea how I'd possibly be a good father. So I came out here, marked some lines in the sand, and started building. Must've been more stressed than I knew, because I built way more than I needed."

Dad looks at his new creation in the third bay and nods to himself. "Only it turned out I didn't," he says. "I just didn't know I'd be building part of it for you one day."

Okay. He needs to stop this before I lose it completely.

"Well, we going to sit here getting gushy?" I ask. "Or we going to try this thing out?"

Dad grins and holds up my helmet and pads, which I now see he's already laid out on the workbench. "What do you think? Time to go pinch it, girl."

I laugh, remembering how he used to toss me over his head to pinch the full moon. Then, as I rush toward the steps at the end, trying to wheel and pull on my helmet at the same time, I notice what's painted on the side of them. Since Dad couldn't draw his way out of a paper bag if his life depended on it, he must've gotten his friend who does airbrushing on cars and motorcycles to paint the design.

A big silver orb, surrounded by sparkly stars and wispy dark clouds. Bold, messy words scrolled right across the top.

Emmie's Moon.

Dad never stopped believing I could grab that moon, did he?

He just needed enough time to build the right launchpad.

33

Testudo Time

I wake up on Saturday morning feeling different. I don't know if I'm still keyed up from finally figuring things out with Dad. Or from the rush of the three hours we spent last night breaking in the new foam pit.

Whatever it is, something's creeping into my headspace. A feeling Mom used to call battle mode. Usually she felt this when she was getting ready for an IEP meeting, but other times, too. Before Dad had a big test, or if she had to go argue with the hospital billing department about a wrong charge. She'd put on certain music—lots of loud, angry strings and shouty voices—to get herself pumped up as she got ready.

Assemble your team.

Gear up.

Raise your flag.

Speaking of *gear*, I've been thinking about that, too. Like when Devontae joked that *the gear doesn't make the athlete* when Mr. Singletary busted on him for wearing rodeo boots on the basketball court.

Only sometimes, the gear actually *does*.

Take that foam pit. I spent three hours sailing off into that thing last night and didn't get a single bruise.

It's given me the faintest glimmer of an idea.

The presentation is tomorrow night.

I've got exactly thirty-six hours to assemble my team, gear up, and raise my flag.

First thing I do is force myself to spend an hour turning Devontae's and my rough notes into a project outline. It's messy, but it's something, and I send it to him before I have time to stress over if I've done a crappy job on it.

Next, I message Ale.

HalfpipeEmms: Congrats on the test, your mom said you aced it. Knew you would.

ApisMelli: Thanks for the cones. How long did they take to pick up?

HalfpipeEmms: Forever.

Then, because I've been learning a lot about the trouble communication—or lack of it—can fix or cause, I swallow hard and tell her I'm sorry. Her reply comes back quick.

ApisMelli: Me too. Besides, we can't still be fighting when you're helping me study for my next test.

Luckily, Ale can't see or hear me groan through the screen at the thought of more bee time. I fill her in about tomorrow and my slowly forming plan. We talk details, and she promises to pass the word to Tina, Zeke, and Markus—and even Logan—about their parts. When we're done talking, I realize that, fight or not, Ale's always right there—whenever I need her, no matter what else she's got going on. As soon as tomorrow's over, I think I've got some brushing up to do in the best friend department.

Then I send another message to Devontae, asking him to fill Shuri in on what's about to go down.

Broncs&Boots: Shuri says she's in. Says thanks for the outline, too—she'll clean it up a little before Monday, but it looks good.

Broncs&Boots: You sure about this, Emmie?

HalfpipeEmms: Yep.

Step one: Assemble your team. Check.

Step two: Gear up.

This one's complicated. I still have that money Nonny gave me for a "suitable dress" sitting in my top drawer, and she's supposed to come over around noon to drive us to town to pick one out, but I have a little something different in mind.

When Nonny arrives to pick me up, I've got the sewing machine set up on the kitchen table and one of

Mom's costume dresses on the chair beside it. When I tell Nonny what I want to do, her first reaction is disapproval. I expected that, and I don't budge.

"This is what I want to wear, Nonny," I tell her. Then, because desperate times, I pull out the zinger. "I want to feel close to Mom tomorrow."

An unfair move maybe, but it works. Nonny closes her mouth mid-protest and sighs. I suddenly realize how much older she looks than she did two years ago. She slowly picks up Mom's dress and runs her fingers along the carefully shredded green fabric on the bodice.

"What was this even supposed to be?"

"A forest fairy," I tell her.

Nonny chuckles. "I always did wonder why God sent a girl like her to a woman like me," she says. "I wish you'd known your mother when she was your age, Emelyn. She'd come home with a stack of books so high she could barely see over them, then burrow up in some corner and disappear into them. Always asking things, coming up with ideas I'd never even heard of, much less knew how to answer. *Brain like a bag of sparks*, that's what your granddaddy always said."

"He was proud of her," I say. Pop-Pop and Mom never tangled like she and Nonny did.

"Of course he was," Nonny says sharply. She pulls off her glasses and rubs her eyes. "So was I. *So* proud of that girl. I was just afraid of what the world would do to a soul like that. I always tried to reel her back down to reality. Remind her she was a Carolina country girl to pull her head out of those clouds a bit. But she always said reality was nothing but *location times imagination*."

I've never heard Nonny talk this way before. I don't know that I will again anytime soon, because she swipes at her eyes once and shoves her glasses back on. Then she catches up the dress in one hand and a pair of scissors in the other.

"All right," she says, her voice jam-full of that same steel I used to hear in Mom's now and then. "So, we need to make this raggedy thing fit you properly?"

When we've finished, Mom's dress fits me perfectly. We leave the sleeves and skirt a bit long, enough fabric to drape over my elbows and knees, and even Nonny can't keep the disapproving look on her face when I try it on.

"Lord," she whispers. "There you go, Emelyn. Reminding me of her so much it hurts."

"I'm sorry," I say, though I can't much help it—or want to—if I'm like Mom.

"Don't be, girl," Nonny says. "Sometimes feeling the hurt is better than not feeling it."

After Nonny leaves, I get out my tool kit and give

my chair a once-over, checking for loose screws or any other damage from all the ramp time I've given it lately.

Step two: Gear up. Check.

Step three: Raise your flag.

Well, I don't have a flag, but Mom used to say that one was more of a metaphor.

Which means, metaphorically, I guess I'm as ready as I'm going to get.

Sure wish my double-flipping stomach would get the message.

34

Team Emmie

As we arrive at the school on Sunday night, I suddenly wish Mom's battle flag wasn't only a metaphor. Because I sure could use one. A battle flag, a pirate flag, an Avengers flag—*something*. Anything but the all-white, give-up-now flag my brain keeps picturing.

The school parking lot is slap *full*.

I try to swat that white surrender flag out of my head, but it latches onto the edge of my thoughts and sits there. Daring me to try and ignore it.

Breathe.

"Emms?" Dad gives me a worried look. "You okay over there?"

I squeeze my eyes shut and tell myself this isn't as scary as facing down a half-pipe, especially before I had a foam-filled landing pit.

It's a lie. I feel like I ate a bunch of live worms.

Overflow parking lines the street on both sides. I see a couple news vans, spitting out people and cameras.

"Emms?" Dad repeats, reaching for my elbow. I get it together and pull it out of range.

"I'm fine. I'm fine."

Can't blame him for the *Who're you kidding?* look. But I'm sticking to my story. I've come this far.

"Not too late to change your mind." Dad glances through the windshield at the people clogging the roadsides and whistles low. "Somehow," he says slowly, "I'm not sure I quite understood how big this thing had got. Did you?"

"Not exactly. Maybe." Dad's not big on the news, and I never told him about the article hung up at school last week, so I'm not shocked he's surprised.

The plan I've been carefully laying out with my friends since yesterday seems a lot more foolish now I actually see how many eyes are going to be on me. I try not to panic as Dad inches through the lot and wonder if I'm about to make the worst mistake of my life.

We reach the school, and Dad cuts the engine and turns in his seat. "Emelyn," he says, slow and serious, "you don't have to do this. Nobody can make you do this. Say the word, we'll drive right out of here. Stop for sundaes, then hit the half-pipe together. I can work some overtime to help you get that chair a little faster."

Same as always, Dad would work himself into a hole for me the best way he knows how, and I love him for it. But, like I screamed at him just before he took a twelve-pound sledge to the old ramp, I'm not a little kid anymore.

I breathe deep, trying to channel as much Mom-style, battle-mode attitude as I can scrape up and grip the bag in my lap. This isn't about the chair anymore.

"Nah," I tell him. "Not backing out now. Don't worry. Gonna be fine."

"Girl, you must be feeling *fine!*"

"Your big night, huh?"

"Emelyn! Can I get a quick statement for the record before things get started?"

The voices and faces blur as I struggle through the crowded main hallway until Dad gets ahead of me and basically bulldozes a path. He barely even notices when he almost sends a few folks sailing into the potted tree at the corner, and we make it up the much quieter short hall to the back of the gym. Mr. Singletary's waiting for us at the backstage door.

"Ale's inside," he tells me. I hug Dad and tell him again that no, he doesn't need to stay. He goes to find Nonny and Pop-Pop before all the seats are gone.

Ale's waiting at the bottom of the short set of steps. We hug each other, and I immediately feel a little better—about our fight being over and what's about to go down.

"You finished it!" she says, looking at my remade green dress. "You look magical."

"Figured a little fairy dust couldn't hurt." I'm only half joking. "How many people are out there?" I'm almost afraid to ask.

"Like, a million!" She grabs my arm. "Looks like half the county!"

That pile of worms in my guts squirms harder.

Ale glances at Mr. Singletary and whispers to me, "You ready?"

"Hope so." Casual as I can, I hand her the bag I've had in my lap. "Are you?"

Getting up the steps isn't bad. Ale and me have done this a million times up the old ramp—this is way easier. I pull myself up using the handrail, and Ale spots me, hauling my chair up behind us. When we're onstage, I peek between the curtains and wish I hadn't. The rows of folding chairs are full, the room humming with voices. The gym's not air-conditioned, and the one big floor fan that's probably a hundred years old groans beside the stage, whipping at top speed but barely cutting the sticky air.

I have a terrible thought.

"What if they seat people right in front of the stage?" I hiss. They've done that when things get crowded before, for plays and award ceremonies—which would ruin everything.

But Ale grins. "Tina got her mom to tell Dr. Grayling it might violate fire codes," she says. "There's plenty of space."

I'm not quite sure if it's relief or dread I feel at knowing the plan is still on.

Ms. Hernandez comes backstage to tell us it's time. There are a few technical glitches—a disconnected mike, twenty seconds where the lights all go out— then things get going. We watch from offstage as Dr. Grayling comes on from the opposite side, welcoming the crowd and thanking everyone who came out two weeks ago and donated. As I listen, I realize two things. One, it honestly was nice of everyone to go to all this effort.

Two—I'm surer than ever of what I need to do.

Then comes a short series of video clips, cast with a projector onto the stage curtain, showing people on wheels doing sports or other cool things. I wanted WCMX clips, of course, and they did use a couple of the ones I suggested. But there are also a bunch Dr. Grayling must have taken himself from some of his mission trips—one is of people in the jungle somewhere being given new wheelchairs by some medical team. There's no sports, but plenty of grateful tears and soppy music.

Not exactly what I would have chosen.

Imagining what AK_SalmonGranny would say about it if she were here makes me feel a little better.

Thankfully, it doesn't last long. Soon, Dr. Grayling's wrapping up, and Ms. Hernandez cues me to go out. We've talked about what comes next—I make a short speech and tell everyone how the money's going to "change my life," and then they hand me a huge cardboard check.

"Don't forget," she whispers as I poke the curtains open. "When Dr. Grayling shakes your hand, hold it a few seconds for the cameras."

My heart's pounding so hard I barely hear her, but I nod and grip my rims hard to keep my hands from shaking. Ale leans over.

"You got this, chica. I'll be ready."

Her voice in my ear calms me a little. "You better," I whisper back, and we fist-bump. Then I breathe deep and go out onto the stage.

The crowd cheers, and I blink in the spotlight as Ms. Hernandez introduces me and then clips a wireless microphone to the neckline of my dress.

Now—*finally*—it's my turn to talk.

I spent hours last night thinking about what to say. How the people in Devontae's and my project might say it if they were making this speech.

But I'm just me—which will have to do.

"This is a lot of money," I start. "And I'm grateful for what it can do." I glance at Dr. Grayling, who's got the big, cardboard check in his hands. He nods approvingly.

"But I think the school got it backward," I continue. "A new chair's been my dream for a long time—one I've been—*am*—working for. My wheels are my freedom, my gear. But what good is new gear if I have to use it at a school with no automatic door or ramps built to code?"

Dr. Grayling's smile freezes.

I hear a few murmurs in the crowd. A flash goes off close by, and a reporter in the front row types furiously on her tablet.

But me, I feel like something is finally thawing out. Pieces melting into place. Maybe I struggled to find the words to explain how I feel to everyone one-to-one, but up here, with the lights in my eyes and the crowd at my feet . . . somehow the words just come.

I fidget with the mike clipped to my dress and keep going, more confident with each word.

"Some of you know I love WCMX—chair skating. That I like to go fast and maybe take a few chances now and then—like any other junior high kid in the world, probably. Most of you at school know I wiped out on that ramp to the portables a few weeks ago, but you probably don't know it was because the ramp wasn't built right for a wheelchair." I decide not to mention Logan's antics or Devontae's belt buckle. "What I want everyone to think about is that *all* kids wipe out now and then—it's what we do. Especially kids who play sports, kids who like to go fast. Using wheels shouldn't have to mean I can't do that sometimes, too, without everyone having a conniption over it."

The crowd's silent, electric. This needs to wrap up, though, before I lose my nerve. I go over to the podium, where Dr. Grayling waits with the check. His face looks stormy, but I smile, nice and calm, and reach to shake his hand.

"Thank you for raising this money for me," I say as he hands the check over. "I appreciate it, and I accept it—but not for my chair. I can earn that myself. What I *can't* do is make my school accessible, for me or for any other kid or teacher who needs it. Or for anyone's grandma or uncle who comes to a basketball game or play and can't get in the front door without help."

The gym is so quiet the fan's *whip-whip* is a roar. Almost like it's pulsing in time with the churning in my stomach. But I manage to keep it calm on the outside.

"That's where this money comes in. I'm donating it back to the school to get started on some accessibility for the main building and the portables, too. We all know funds are tight and there's plenty needs doing."

Then I push that check back into Dr. Grayling's hand. He's so shocked he actually takes it.

The gym goes cemetery still, except the thrum of that big, ancient fan and the photo flashes of a hundred phones. The fan is close enough that I feel a ghost of air shift across my face. The whooshing of those big metal blades is like a fast-moving heartbeat. Like when you're scared or mad . . .

Or poised at the top of a jump.

Then one of the heavy doors at the gym entrance slams shut, crashing so loud everyone jumps and turns to look.

That'd be Tina. Playing magician, pulling the audience's attention from where the real action's going down.

It's my cue. Emmie *out*.

It only distracts everyone for a few confused seconds, but that's all I need.

I slip into my zone, let myself fall into that familiar slice of space. Brain switches off; body takes over. Fast as a shadow, I whip halfway around, ignoring the rising murmur of the crowd, to the edge of the curtain where Ale waits, hidden barely out of sight with my red helmet in her hands.

Ale's my pit crew. Quick as a bee sting, she pushes the helmet onto my head, and I clip the chin strap a half second later.

I don't think.

I *move*.

Hands on wheels. Spin back around. Shove hard, hurtling over the stage. Gathering speed and launching right off the edge.

Whoosh. Wheels. Adrenaline.

One glorious moment of wind rushing around me.

One impossible beat of weightlessness.

Air.

Then, the fall.

Back wheels, then front, kiss the floor.

Landing smack on the thin wrestling mat Markus sneaked onto the floor in front of the stage when the lights "malfunctioned" earlier. Exactly like I asked, he's played sweeper for me, in case this ended up being one of the hundreds of times I lost control of a landing.

But it isn't.

I don't land on my head, or the knee or elbow pads I've got hidden under the long, flowy sleeves and skirt of Mom's made-over green fairy dress.

Oh my *God*—I *did* it.

I hear Ale let loose a victory yell.

It's a toss-up who's more shocked—me or the stunned-silent crowd.

I don't stop to figure it out. I keep moving, shoving hard to get my chair off the mat onto the smooth floor and flying up the aisle between the packed rows of folding chairs. The crowd explodes from shocked silence to wild applause.

On cue, Zeke and Devontae slip out of aisle seats and jog with me. They're my testudo, making sure nobody gets in my way. Shouts, whistles, and flashes erupt around us like fireworks, shaking the gym like a little storm. Questions are already flying at me from both sides, but I ignore it all and push harder.

We race to the door, which opens right on cue. Logan's holding it, and even going this fast, I see the grin about to split his face in two. Asking him to be my escape hatch was a last-minute decision, but I can't help grinning back as I sail through the door into the hallway.

"You *killed* it!" Zeke says when the door bangs shut behind us, abruptly muffling—but not completely quieting—the roar of the crowd.

Tina and Ale appear from opposite directions, Ale out of breath from running down two hallways. She doesn't stop until she crashes into me and hugs me so hard we almost tip over. "You flew like a fairy," she whispers, and I poke her for being so goofy.

"She's right," Devontae says. "That was amazing."

"That what Shuri said?" I joke.

"Yeah. And me." He drops his voice lower and adds, "I think I get it now."

Good thing my face was already flushed. Nobody'll notice one more blush.

Surrounded by Team Emmie and fresh off the rush of the gutsiest—or most fool-headed—thing I've ever done in public, I feel like I can take on the world. I pull off my helmet and smooth down my hair.

Then the door swings open again, and people flow into the hall like a flash flood. Dr. Grayling's at the front of the pack, mad as heck, and I wonder which of the stunts I pulled has him more fired up. He starts toward us, mouth already open.

"Uh-oh," Zeke says, and I realize with a sinking feeling that when I imagined how this would go, I was so focused on how I'd even make it off that stage I didn't think enough about how it might all go *after*.

Then I look behind him—at that crowd all going wild with excitement over what I just did—and that sinking feeling . . . stops, as the weight of it all hits me.

I got up there. Spoke up for myself. Nailed the best

jump of my life *off the stage*, in front of *everyone*. With my raggedy old wheelchair, no less.

One little Fish isn't going to get the best of me now.

I don't wait for him to reach us. I roll across the hall to meet him, pulling up so close my footrests almost touch his shiny shoes, and tilt my head back to meet his eyes.

"Some crowd, huh? Did you see me stick that landing?"

He wasn't expecting that, and he pauses. Maybe I'm still riding the adrenaline rush or maybe I've just gotten braver, because I finally find the courage to be honest.

"I'm not a cause," I tell him. "I'm a kid. And an athlete. Same as all your other students."

As irritated as I've been with him through this, the confusion on Dr. Grayling's face makes me feel a tiny bit bad for him. He was so sure he was doing everything right here.

I can tell he's still not convinced, and he opens his mouth to argue. But then two sets of people reach either side of us at almost the same second.

On one side are Dad, Nonny, and Pop-Pop. Dad's shaking his head, trying and completely failing to look mad at me instead of so proud he might explode.

On the other, four newspeople skid to a stop so fast

one almost trips over a folded tripod. They hurry over to where Dr. Grayling and I are facing off, questions already flying.

"Emmie! That was incredible!"

"Dr. Grayling? Could we get your thoughts about the school accessibility issue?"

"Have you consulted with local disability agencies about this problem?"

Fish freezes. He looks from me to the cameras and back again. His mouth opens and closes a few times like a bass testing the bait, and I'm 90 percent certain I've finally won this battle.

But a deep-down, ornery part of me has to make sure.

I pop into a smooth wheelie and hold it, my front wheels floating and the cameras rolling. Like I've said, it's a lot easier than it looks, but none of them have to know that. Dr. Grayling and I lock eyes again as the flashes and questions flurry around us, and I give him a smile that's actually real.

One that *dares* him to tell me to stop.

35

Case Closed

BUDDING ACTIVIST ISSUES CHALLENGE OVER SCHOOL ACCESSIBILITY

Charles Hubbard, Staff Reporter

(Lakeville, SC) A Lakeville junior high student threw down an unexpected challenge to members of her school and community on Sunday night at E. L. Pinckney Junior High School. When Emelyn Ethrige, age 12, took the stage, the audience expected to see her receive a community-donated check to cover the cost of a new custom wheelchair. But, in a surprise twist, Emelyn gave the money back to the school, asking them to put it toward making her school campus accessible "for me and other folks here who use wheels."

If that wasn't enough of a surprise, the audience was abruptly shocked—then dazzled—when Emelyn suddenly launched her wheelchair off the edge of the stage. A budding wheelchair-stunt enthusiast, Emelyn made a perfect landing and then left the event surrounded by her friends, leaving the crowd cheering. When asked what inspired her to do this, Emmie shrugged. "Sometimes you just want to show what you can do. Ask any athlete."

When asked whether he felt the school buildings' current level of accessibility was sufficient, or how many students and staff at ELPJHS would potentially benefit from improved architectural accessibility, Dr. Bruce Grayling, principal at ELPJHS, said he would "be certainly looking into the matter."

According to several school board members who were in the audience, the accessibility issue will be on the agenda at next month's board meeting. Community input is welcomed.

"Your dad's going to kill us, Emmie," Ale says cheerfully as she unloads a stack of beekeeping supplies onto one end of the longest new worktable.

"Nope." I finish trimming the piece of fabric in my hand and set the scissors down. "Not this time. Was his idea."

Ale and I are trying out the brand-new workspace in the shop that Dad helped us set up. It's got long, low tables, stacked and labeled plastic totes, and even one of his big tool chests, freshly cleaned and emptied of tools. Plenty of storage for supplies for our shop, plus loads of space to spread out and work. Dad said that with as hard as Ale and me have been going at it, the least he could do was help us with some better infrastructure. Especially since he can't exactly work in three shop bays at once.

Same old Dad. Always the logistics guy.

The new spot's perfect, though. Ale and I already have our wall thermometers hung up, and pictures of my wheels and her beehive to help keep us motivated.

"How much longer you think it's going to take us?" Ale asks, as if she's read my mind.

I ball up a fabric scrap and toss it at her. "Depends how much time I'm going to be spending with you and those bee books." Going to have to get to work on that bee fear of mine, too.

Ale looks pointedly over at the half-pipe across the work bay—my biggest rush and worst temptation by far these days. Good thing Devontae and me managed to scrape a B-minus on our project proposal . . . and have a few more weeks to write the final presentation.

"Okay, okay." I give in. "We'll keep each other motivated."

Ale takes a closer look at the latest wheelchair bag I'm piecing out. "Another cusswords one?" She raises her eyebrows. "I thought you gave those up?"

"I did," I tell her, then explain I'm sending this one as a gift to a certain island in Alaska. To thank a certain cuss-loving, salmon-catching grandma for giving me some good advice when I needed it. She was right about a lot of things—I do need to find my voice in my own way, which isn't exactly the same as hers. Or my mom's. Or anyone's but mine.

I don't need cusswords on my bag, but I do need words. Strong ones.

My own.

I'll keep working on it.

In the meantime, I've shifted gears on the wheelchair bags I'm still making toward a more cosplay/fantasy theme. I got the idea from some of the costumes we saw at the Fairy Festival, and they're selling good so far. So are the skater-themed ones.

Of course, there's always those never-ending packages of pine cones and Spanish moss to keep us nice and sticky.

"I still can't believe you pulled it off," Ale says as she counts out pine cones and scoops them into gallon-size ziplocks. "I'm so bummed I couldn't see Fish's face the moment you sailed off that stage."

It was a big risk I took. Probably bordering on foolish, if I'm honest.

But hey. What almost-thirteen-year-old doesn't pull some fool-headed stunts now and then?

The gamble paid off. With the news cameras catching every minute of my speech—not to mention my perfect jump and landing—Dr. Grayling didn't have much wiggle room when all those questions started coming in about why more hadn't been done to make E. L. Pinckney wheelchair accessible before now.

Talk about optics.

I suspect all those cameras being right there—and the way the crowd went for it—is what kept me out of some serious trouble at school for pulling that stunt at all. We'll see what he meant when he said they'd "look into the architecture matter promptly."

I know they've got at least $2,678 to get them started.

I was a little worried what Devontae's family might think, given their big donation for what they thought was my new chair. But when they came up to congratulate me after the ceremony, all of them—including Momma Rose—gave me huge hugs.

Best of all, I've got my freedom back at school. Speaking up must be contagious or something, because before we even left school that night, Dad made a point to find Ms. Hernandez and Dr. Grayling and inform them I would no longer be needing an aide at school. Case closed.

I felt a little bad about Dawn losing her job, but it turned out okay. Seems she'd always wanted to do more with that scrapbooking hobby of hers, and hearing about our online shop got her thinking. Not only that, but Ale's aunt Rosaria—the one who makes custom dresses for weddings and quinces and other fancy events—saw the beautiful scrapbook Dawn donated for the raffle and bought a boatload of tickets for it. Not only did she win it, she liked it so much she asked Dawn if she'd make special, event-themed ones to sell in her dress shop and on her website.

Last I heard, orders were already piling up. I ran into Dawn at Dollar General again—both of us in the art supplies section this time—and when I asked how it was going, she looked excited about being an entrepreneur and grateful she doesn't have to leave her mom home alone anymore. "You really inspired me, Emmie" is what she said.

For once, someone saying that *finally* felt like something worth hearing.

36

Worth the Wait

It's not a date.

It's a boring old winter dance. Everybody goes. All seven of us are meeting in a group in the parking lot and going in together. Then we'll probably hang out together most of the evening. No big thing.

Can I help it if Devontae happens to be waiting by himself at the curb when we pull up in front of the school? Or that we've been hanging together more and more in the almost three months since I flipped that awards ceremony onto its head?

Ale reaches over the seat and pokes my shoulder. "Uh-huh," she whispers. "Just all going as friends. *Sure.*"

I poke her back, nodding at my dad in the driver seat and giving her a *Hush up!* look. Dad's eyebrows go up, but he shakes his head.

"How about I pretend I didn't hear that," he says.

"We'll talk about it when you're thirty. Maybe thirty-five. Have fun, Emms." He leans over to give me a quick hug.

I roll down the window as Dad climbs out and goes to the bed for my wheels. "Fancy running into you here, Boots." I hope I sound a whole lot cooler than I feel.

Devontae's wearing a silver-trimmed black shirt and boots to match. Looking handsomer than anyone should. "I love coincidence." He opens my door with a grin. "Don't you?"

"Shuri says you look nice," he adds in a whisper. Then he sees what my dad has unloaded from the bed and whistles.

"Daaang," he says, drawing it out. "You weren't kidding about that new ride of yours. Worth the wait, in*deed*."

It totally was, and I feel a grin, proud and happy, spread over my face. Dad parks my new chair beside the truck, and I swing down into it, smoothing my fluffy skirt over my knees. I've cut down another one of Mom's costume dresses to fit me, and I'm especially pleased with this one. It's shimmery silver, like snow and smoke mixed together, and the spangles on the skirt catch the light from inside the school like tiny rainbows.

We all tell my dad bye and head up the pavement

toward the school, where the rest of our friends are waiting. Logan, of course, is the first with something to say.

"Wow," he says, looking over the new chair. "Did you get green and red for Christmas? Can you get different colors for every holiday?"

Everyone groans, and Tina pokes him. "It's *Poison Apple*," she says, like it's obvious. "And she got it because it's *amazing*."

Logan looks a little squashed, but I can't help joining in the laughing. Now that he's gotten the message that help's only help if someone wants it, Logan's growing on me. Sort of like an intriguing fungus. Tina's right about the chair colors, though. All the rest of it, too. It *is* amazing.

It took two more months' hard work, sewing chair bags and chopping and tying sappy little firewood bundles and wrestling stringy Spanish moss into plastic bags. But I did it.

I earned the money and got my new chair all by myself.

It's glorious. Knobby-tire, beastly framed, Kevlar-cushion perfection.

I've spent so much time all week cruising and flipping and wiping out in my new foam pit in the shop, testing to see what this chair can really do, Dad jokes he never would've built it in the first place if he'd known he was going to lose his assistant mechanic over it.

He was only messing. We both know I'm going to be helping him out more than ever here soon, because he's headed back to night classes next week. We'll get it done somehow. Dad says maybe he'll be able to focus on studying now he's not burning half his headspace stressing about my crashing off that raggedy old ramp out in the field.

"You really did it." Zeke crouches down and looks appreciatively at the chair's undercarriage. "This thing is sway. Wish I had me a bike that solid."

"Bet you could earn one if you put your mind to it," Ale says. She looks proud, too, and I think about the fun we had last week, when she reached her goal and I helped her put in her order for that fancy beehive. It'll get here in two weeks. Good thing I'm making headway on that bee fear of mine, because Lord knows I'll be helping her get it all set up come spring.

"Nice ride!" someone calls behind me. I turn just in time to see Demarion zip past at max speed. I laugh as he disappears into the school with a group of his artsy friends.

"So, are you both done with the e-shop now, girls?"

Tina asks. "Now that y'all have smashed all those lofty goals you set way back last summer?"

Ale and I trade glances. "Nah . . ." she says slowly. "What fun's smashing a goal if you don't have another one in the works?"

I know she's already thinking ahead to the next level of beekeeper certification—journeyman—and I grin back. Me, I'm thinking about the label on the brand-new coffee can sitting on the corner of my desk.

Sports Camp!!! ☺ ☺ ☺

No, it's not the Tate Britain in London. Not for now. What it *is*, is an adaptive sports camp out in California, which feels almost as far away in some ways. But it's an adaptive sports camp that offers all sorts of unbelievable chair sports. Hockey. Canoeing. Basketball.

And WCMX.

No secret which one I'm shooting for. I can't wait.

We're almost at the front door now, and Devontae has fallen into step beside me. When his fingers maybe-probably-*almost*-accidentally brush against mine, I maybe-probably-*almost*-accidentally catch hold of his pinky and lace my own back through his.

Only for a second. Just long enough to let him know I mean it.

"Hold up." I reach out and stop him when we get close to the door. "Let me do the honors."

He stops, and I push past him on my beautiful, brand-new wheels, right up to that beautiful, brand-new automatic door that now graces the front of E. L. Pinckney Junior High.

I never in a million years thought I'd quote old Principal Fish, but he got one thing right.

Goes to show what a small community can do when it sets its mind to it.

The door whooshes open, letting out the thump of music, the chatter of voices, and a rush of air that smells like a mash-up of gingerbread, sweat, and peppermint.

I breathe deep, feeling that air on my face.

Then, without even having to slow down or fumble a handle, I lead the way inside.

Author's Note

The right to an education wasn't always legally protected for students with disabilities in the United States—and still isn't in many parts of the world. In 1973, Section 504 of the Rehabilitation Act was signed into law, becoming the first federal civil rights protection for people with disabilities in this country. But laws don't always mean immediate change, and the disability community continued to fight for equal rights for years to come—and still does today. In 1977, frustrated with lack of progress, disabled activists and allies staged a four-week sit-in of a federal building in San Francisco to insist that legislators implement the regulations needed to protect the rights of people with disabilities to have fair and equal access to schools, universities, and other areas enjoyed by the public. This demonstration brought people together from many different cultures, economic backgrounds, and ages, united by the common cause of equality regardless of ability. Demonstrations spread to other cities around the country, including Washington, DC, New York, Denver, Boston, Seattle, and many others.

Today students with disabilities in the United States have legally protected rights. Public schools in all fifty states must comply with the Individuals with Disabilities Education Act (IDEA) of 2004, which requires schools to provide a free and equal public education to students of all abilities. Classroom accommodations, specialized instruction, specialist services like physical or occupational therapy, and one-to-one aides are examples of important supports that may be provided for students with additional needs.

But what if help—however well-meaning—becomes less than helpful? In *Air*, Emmie is confronted with a subtle, often overlooked problem. Individualized educational plans and 504 plans are crucial tools that help many children with disabilities—and their families— have fair and equal access to education. But occasionally, well-intentioned accommodation programs—and those who create them—can inadvertently limit kids more than necessary.

As a pediatric physical therapist, I look at what children who have disabilities can physically do—with or without help—and also when the architecture around them isn't suited to their needs. Once, while working for a rural school district, I was asked to weigh in on whether a certain junior high student needed a one-to-one aide during the school day. His teachers and the principal felt he did. The student was adamant that he didn't, while his parents were undecided. I was asked to be the tiebreaker, which led me to consider a complicated question. Was this student fully independent at school with his wheelchair?

It depended on how you looked at it. This student was a lifelong wheelchair user who was physically active and dreamed of one day joining a wheelchair basketball team. Like many other active junior high students, he liked to go fast and take a few chances here and there. He was quite independent and could easily get through most of his school day without extra help. But the ramp he had to use to reach some of his classes was too steep, with warped floorboards and a sticky, splinter-filled railing. The one bathroom large enough to accommodate his wheelchair did not have grab bars or other adaptations that would have made it easier and safer for him to use it without help. The only times he had trouble were when he had to navigate situations where the school building had not been built to properly accommodate a wheelchair, yet for this particular school—located in a disadvantaged area with limited resources—it had felt more feasible to hire an aide than to modify the school's architecture to enable him to get around fully independently.

In the end, I suggested a compromise—the student

and I would work together on strategies for helping him go up and down the ramp a little more safely (he did like speed, after all!), while the school would make repairs to the ramp and add grab bars in the bathroom. The student liked this idea, and he and I made a long-term goal for him to work toward not having an aide at school. This is in no way intended to discount the crucial supports provided by dedicated aides to many, many students who have specific needs while at school. But in this student's case, I felt that better architecture—not someone helping him all day long—was the best and fairest accommodation for what he both wanted and needed.

Like this student, Emmie is an active, athletic young person who happens to ride on wheels. And, like this student, Emmie confronts struggles that stemmed mostly from a built environment that wasn't designed or constructed with her needs in mind—and from what people around her wrongly assumed she could or couldn't do.

Acknowledgments

So many people helped this book take flight. A mountain of thanks to my amazing agent, Jacqui Lipton. You took a most unexpected chance on me, and I'm forever grateful. Sincere gratitude to Wes Adams, Melissa Warten, Brian Luster, Helen Seachrist, and the rest of the FSG team for your enthusiasm, wisdom, and vision. I couldn't ask for a better editorial home. Thanks to Mallory Grigg and Oriol Vidal for a book design and jacket art beyond my dreams. Thanks to Cindie Gillis and Alex Blaszczuk for thoughtful and insightful authenticity reads.

Thank you to the wonderful faculty, staff, and students/alumnx (especially my Darling Assassins) of Vermont College of Fine Arts. Writing may be a solitary endeavor, but Brigadoon helps ensure it needn't be a lonely one.

Tirzah Price, you are the kindest, funniest, most fiercely loyal critique partner and friend. Here's to more books, postcards, and launch-day MSCs. To my dearly irreverent Birches, for margaritas, beach rambles, and (our buddy) Wicker Man. To Kate and Cassie

Beasley for writing weekends, surprise snake battles, and helpful critiques. To Mara Wolf, for help with early details, and Tanisha Brown and K. E. Lewis for insightful full-draft feedback. To my Saturday-morning crew (Tanisha, K.E., James Williams, and Tee Moore) for feedback, friendship, and fun.

Thanks to Ellen, Eric, Connor, and Kate, for letting us crash in the Fairy Tower, crash your Zooms, and haunt your kitchen during revisions, pandemic parenting, and other mad sundries. Hope the ghost hunts, bladder serenades, and rainbow bread made it memorable. Thanks, Mom, for finding boxfuls of yard-sale books and never censoring what was in them. In those tight times when books were my escape, you made sure I had piles of them. Thanks, Dad, for afternoons in the woodshop that led to good talks.

Mr. Francisco Cal, thank you for shared lunches beside dozens of rivers and your passionate advocacy for inclusive education. To the activists, advocates, and allies—past and present—who've worked tirelessly to promote the social model of disability and educational access in communities around the world.

Sincere thanks to the kids, families, teachers, and support staff I've been honored to work with, learn from, and advocate for—and to the trailblazers of

WCMX and other adaptive sports that push boundaries, upend expectations, and help kids dream big.

Lastly—most importantly—to David and Raven. We're three stubborn peas who fight hard and love harder. Thanks for waking me with coffee in bed and slipping dinner onto my desk when I'm grumpily flailing through a draft. Wouldn't want to share my pod with anyone else.